JAKE'S TREASURE

Where his branch joined the main trunk there was a thick mass of vegetation which looked as though it might be concealing a hole. With the torch held in his mouth, pointing forward and lit, he parted the plants with his hands and looked in. It seemed to be a kind of nest made of bamboo leaves and twigs. When he pointed the torch down to the bottom he saw that he was right. There was a pile of whitish eggs. They seemed big and there were an awful lot of them. For a moment Jake wondered what sort of bird they could possibly belong to. Then, in the same instant, he heard the hissing and saw the hatchlings. They were not chicks at all; they were little cobras. There were about half a dozen that had hatched and they were unmistakable; perfect miniature replicas of the parents he had been following. Two or three had their tiny hoods raised and were ready to strike.

JAKE'S TREASURE

by

ROBIN HANBURY-TENISON

RED FOX

For Merlin

A Red Fox Book

Published by Random House Children's Books
20 Vauxhall Bridge Road, London SW1V 2SA

A division of Random House UK Ltd
London Melbourne Sydney Auckland
Johannesburg and agencies throughout the world

Copyright © Robin Hanbury-Tenison 1998

1 3 5 7 9 10 8 6 4 2

First published in Great Britain by Red Fox 1998

Typeset in Great Britain by SX Composing DTP, Rayleigh, Essex
Printed and bound in Great Britain by
Cox & Wyman Ltd., Reading Berkshire

Papers used by Random House UK Limited are natural, recyclable
products made from wood grown in sustainable forest. The
manufacturing processes conform to the environmental regulations
of the country of origin.

RANDOM HOUSE UK Limited Reg No. 954009

ISBN 0 09 925625 8

1
Granny Maisy

Jake's grandmother seemed much older than she really was. Sometimes she was just like a normal granny, but, like many old people, she could get confused, lose the thread of what she was saying or even tail off in the middle of a sentence. She would often ask Jake about life on the farm where he lived with his mother and stepfather; about Farmer Thomas next door, whom she had known when he was a child; and about the games Jake and Keith Thomas, the farmer's son, played in the fields and woods near their homes. Then, suddenly, she would start talking about something completely different, ending up mumbling and gazing into space.

At first, Jake had found it embarrassing going to see her now she was like this, but then, as she didn't seem to mind or even to remember the nonsense she often made of a conversation, he decided that he wouldn't mind either but would concentrate instead on listening to the good bits.

And there were plenty of them if you listened carefully. Granny Maisy had led an interesting life. Widowed in India at the very end of the Second World War, just before Jake's mother, her only child, was born, she had returned to England, trained as a secretary and worked in lots of different jobs. Working hard while bringing up a child had been tough, but when her daughter had grown up, left home to study art and finally got a job of her own, she had been able to do what she had always wanted to do – travel.

She had had lots of adventures and Jake loved to hear about them. The fact that they usually had no beginning or end just made them more fascinating. Sometimes he told her about the great adventure he had had when he was lost in the Amazon jungle and rescued by an Indian tribe*.

Granny Maisy now lived in a sheltered home in the village where Jake went to school. She could look after herself but Jake's mum felt happier knowing there were people around to help her if she needed them. She had suggested that Granny Maisy moved in with them but she preferred to pretend she was still independent.

On his way back to school one evening in the summer term a year after his Amazon adven-

*Jake's Escape

ture, Jake dropped in on his granny and found her half asleep.

'Hello darling,' she said, 'I was dreaming.'

'What about?' asked Jake.

'Oh about when I was younger and went out to India to be married.'

'Do tell me about it, Granny,' Jake begged. He knew very little about that part of her life as she seldom talked about it.

'Well, I'll try,' she answered, 'but you know what my memory's like now.'

'I'm glad she doesn't realize how bad it really is!' thought Jake sadly to himself. Then, out loud, he said, 'Go on Gran, just the bits you were dreaming.'

'First there was the boat. It was a great big ocean liner and because I was on my way to my wedding I travelled POSH. Do you know what that means?'

'First Class, I suppose,' answered Jake.

'No it doesn't. We were all one class and very luxurious it was, too, before the War. POSH stands for Port Out, Starboard Home. Port is the left side of the boat and Starboard is the right. It was smart to be on the side away from the sun as there was no air conditioning in those days and the cabin got very hot if the sun shone into them. So it was best to be on the left on the way out to India and on the right on the way home. England was always 'Home'.

3

'Then there was the train. I had lots of luggage and I travelled for days and days right across India. It was very hot. But I loved Dangma from the moment I first saw it. That was the tea plantation in Assam which your grandfather managed and I was so happy there for seven years with him.' Jake saw his granny's eyes go cloudy and fill with tears.

'So sad,' she said, 'so sad.' And that was all he could get out of her that afternoon.

Over the next few weeks he teased more of the story out of her. Sudden flashes of memory came when she described the big green-roofed bungalow with fine polished wooden floors and big fans to cool the air, operated by a boy called a punkah wallah, who sat pulling a string which made the fan flap.

There were stories of rides on elephants to hunt tigers which had taken someone from one of the villages around the plantation. These tigers were man-eaters which had usually been injured or lost their teeth and so turned to the easiest prey – man, or more usually woman or child – and so had to be shot.

There were treks high into the Himalayas, where snow-capped peaks could be seen on clear days. During the hot months they had gone up there to get away from the intense heat of the plains. She described Buddhist monasteries, old Lama hermits with long straggly hair living naked at snow level in caves. But whenever she mentioned her husband, George, she would start to go all dreamy and weepy and Jake would have to wait for more until the next time.

It was when Granny Maisy first mentioned the Japanese army that she began to behave really strangely. 'It was awful,' was all she would say at first and Jake had to beg her to tell him more. Then, one evening, it all came out in such a rush that Jake could barely follow what she was saying and had to strain to listen as, every now and then, she lost her thread. But he dared not interrupt now the tap had been turned on and he just tried desperately to remember as he felt it was important and possibly the only time he would be told the story.

2
The Japanese Army

'We had heard they were coming for weeks,'
Granny Maisy began, 'and we were all very
frightened. The war had been going badly and
it looked as though India was going to be
invaded. George had been taken on by the
military as a special adviser, since he knew so
much about the country and the people, and he
was almost never at home. Other units kept
passing through, camping in the plantation,
wrecking the tea bushes and moving on. The
poor boys who were invalided out looked awful.
They were thin and haggard with terrible sores
which wouldn't heal. I helped in the hospital . . .
but I couldn't do much as, at last, after waiting
seven years, I was going to have a baby – your
mother.

'George arrived in the middle of the night.
He was covered in mud and exhausted. There
was a small tin box with him which he said was
very important and the servants mustn't see it.
(Everyone in India had servants in those days.)

He had been up in the hills on the Burmese border, close to where the Japanese were sending their scouts and it had been very dangerous. He wouldn't tell me what had happened. Said it was better I didn't know. That the baby was what mattered and he had made arrangements for me to leave. I didn't want to go but he said I must – for the baby's sake. And then he went back into the hills and they came and told me I had to go. It was terrible, terrible. I was so frightened.'

'What happened to the tin box?' asked Jake.

'George said I must hide it and I did. He said it was important . . . but I never saw him again. Terrible, terrible . . .' and she began to mumble.

Try as he might, Jake could not get her to tell him any more and when, later, he raised the subject again she always shut him up, saying, 'I don't want to talk about it.' But Jake had decided that the box held treasure and that one day he was going to go and find it. He thought he would probably have to wait for years before he had the chance to go to India but he began to dream about the country, reading stories about the days of the British Raj, *The Jungle Book* and anything else he could get his hands on.

Just before the end of the summer term, his father came to see him.

'I'm afraid there's no chance of our having a holiday together this year,' he told Jake. 'You'll have lots of fun here on the farm, though. There'll be the harvest soon, and haymaking.'

Jake was disappointed. Although he loved it at home, he always looked forward to his father's sudden arrivals, which often led to an unexpected holiday. He could never quite make out what his father did, except that it involved a lot of travelling to strange places and sometimes he gave lectures.

'Anyway,' his father went on, 'after last time, I'm not sure your mother would be too keen on your going anywhere exciting with me.'

'But where are you going,' Jake asked plaintively, 'and why can't I come, too?'

'I've got to do a month's lecturing in Calcutta. It's an awful place and there would be nothing for you to do there. I'm going to be very busy and there won't be time for any trips into other parts of India.'

Jake realized with a shock that the thing he wanted to do most in the world was suddenly within his grasp. Trying to sound relaxed and as though it didn't matter dreadfully, he said, 'But Dad, I'd really like to come and I promise I won't be any trouble. I never get to see you and we could have lots of fun even if you are busy. Perhaps I could go and stay on a tea plantation. Granny's been telling me about the one she lived on before Mum was born.'

'Well, I don't know . . . I'm not sure it's a good

idea and I doubt if your mother would agree. We can ask her but I wouldn't get your hopes up. I'm not going to push for it after the trouble last time. It's more than my life's worth!'

At first Jake didn't think there was any chance that he would be able to persuade his parents to let him go. They were united in their determination not to let him, especially after all the worry they had been put through the previous year when he had gone missing in the Amazon. But gradually, by using all the arguments he could think of, like how educational it would be and how much he wanted to see the country his mother was born in, he thought they were beginning to weaken.

'He has been spending a lot of time with my mother, which has been very good of him as she is getting awfully vague . . . and I know she's told him lots about her life in India. Let's write and see what the people out there have to say about it. I don't suppose they'll want to have anything to do with us. In a way, I hope they don't. I'd rather like to have him here this holidays.'

And so a letter was sent to the British company which still owned Dangma tea plantation asking if the grandson of the last British manager, who had died defending it from the Japanese, would be allowed to go for a visit. Surprisingly quickly, and to the amazement of them all, an answer came back saying that

George Beckett and his courage were still remembered by some in the company and of course Jake was welcome. He could hardly believe his luck, but his mother was still dubious and insisted on meeting one of their representatives in London, finding out exactly where Jake would be going and making sure that everything would be taken care of.

'He told me that Dangma tea plantation now has an Indian manager, Mr Barua, and that he has a son of Jake's age. It does sound as though they really do want to have him and they have promised that he will be well looked after,' Jake's mother said, and then turning to Jake, she added, 'I'm not at all sure we're making the right decision and you must promise to keep out of trouble. I couldn't take another drama!'

After that, it was plain sailing and arrangements were made for him to fly out with his father at the start of the holidays, which left time for them to get all the necessary permits and injections. And his mother and father finalized the details of Jake's stay at the plantation, with the tea company.

Jake went to tell his grandmother his exciting news, but she seemed not to take it in and whenever he mentioned India or Dangma, she just muttered, 'Terrible terrible . . .' He begged her to tell him where she had hidden the tin box and, for a brief moment, her eyes cleared and she looked straight at him. 'In the garden,' she said. 'In the big . . .' and then her eyes lost their focus and she started to cry so that Jake thought he had better go. He kissed her and said he would give her love to India.

3
India

Much to his surprise, in spite of, or perhaps because he had been in a state of high excitement for days before, Jake slept for most of the long flight to Calcutta. He awoke very early in the morning and looked around the big cabin of the Boeing 747. Rows and rows of people lay slumped in their seats, sprawled in strange positions and covered in blankets, some with their heads back and their mouths open. One good thing, thought Jake, is that you can't hear the snoring over the sound of the engines!

He was in a window seat and he slipped up the plastic blind over the oval window next to him and peered out into the night. It was all dark at first, the stars clear above and nothing but fluffy white clouds in the moonlight below. Then, just as he was about to pull the blind down again and try for some more sleep, he saw a break in the clouds and dark landscape with occasional twinkling lights far, far below. The clouds ended and he could see the curve of the horizon between the black land and the slightly paler sky. Wow, he thought, I never realized that you could see that the world is round from up here.

The world seemed very small from so high up. He had flown 6000 miles, a quarter of the way around the world in a matter of hours. Soon they would be landing at Calcutta . . . Then he saw the Himalayas. The first sun of the morning was catching the snowy peaks and, as the plane turned slightly, the whole magnificent range swung into view. It was, thought Jake, the most beautiful sight he had ever seen. Range after range of vast mountains, each higher than the one in front, seemed to stretch back into the distance for ever. The lower ranges were still in darkness and so only the splendid white summits caught the sun in a dazzling array. Jake glanced at his father, sound asleep beside him, and decided he had to share the moment.

'Wake up, Dad!' he whispered in his ear. 'You have to look at this. It's fantastic!' It was indeed, like some incredible Disney creation, too extravagant for nature to have created it by accidental movements of the earth's crust over millions of years.

After a first cross grunt, Peter Travis opened his eyes wide but, when he saw what Jake was looking at, he leaned eagerly across his son to see if he could recognize any of the peaks.

'We must be just about passing Nepal,' he said after a while. 'I think I recognized Annapurna back there, which means Everest should be coming up soon.' A stewardess, seeing they were awake, brought them glasses of orange juice and leaned across to have a look out of the window, too. 'It never fails to thrill me, that sight, however often I fly this route,' she said. 'There's Everest now, that very white mountain back behind the others, but quite distinct.' And so they stared silently at the highest mountain in the world and Jake held his breath, willing himself to store the moment. It might well be the only time in his life he would see it and he was unlikely to have a better view.

'Phew! That was great, Dad,' he said at last. 'How much longer before we land?'

'A couple of hours, I should think,' his father replied, and they had time to eat breakfast, wash the sleep out of their eyes and stretch their legs with a quick walk up the aisle before starting the descent to Calcutta.

Now Jake stared out of the window again. India looked brown and parched below. Rivers meandered through the plains and there were roads and small houses everywhere. As they dropped lower they could see lots of little square fields which seemed to be flooded as the sun glinted on the surface of the water.

'Why do they do that?' asked Jake. 'Has there

been a flood?'

'No,' his father replied. 'That's rice being grown in padi fields. At just the right moment for the rice to be planted, the water is carefully brought along canals and let into the fields, which are all at slightly different levels and dead flat. Look! There are some people working now, putting each plant in by hand.'

'It must be very hard work,' said Jake.

'It is. Backbreaking. But it's worth it as, if all goes well, you can get three crops in a year.'

'Where are we going to stay again, Dad?' Jake asked.

'With an old friend of mine called Bob,' his father replied. 'I'll tell you about him; he's one of the most unusual people I know. Ten years ago he worked for an international bank and was making lots of money. Then he was sent to the Calcutta branch and, almost by accident, he found out about the railway children.' Jake saw that his father's face had become taut and he looked and sounded grim. 'Every year, thousands of orphaned or abandoned children from all over India find their way to Calcutta's main railway station, called Howrah. Some are as young as four or five and no one really knows why they end up here, but they do. Somehow they survive by begging and stealing, but terrible things happen to them and most die very young. Bob started helping one or two of them to escape from the squalor and try to make a better life for themselves. He gave up his job at the bank and started a school and a home for them. That's where we're going to stay. I'm going to help out when I'm not lecturing in return for my keep. Bob is amazing. He manages to run the whole show brilliantly on almost nothing by getting everyone to help.'

Calcutta from the air was pretty: an endless scatter of houses networked by canals and roads crowded with people and traffic. Once on the ground, it was very different. As soon as they left the airport in an ancient rickety taxi with shiny plastic seats that stuck to their bodies, the heat and the smells hit them. There were people on foot, on bicycles, pulling handcarts and driving cars and trucks everywhere. Jake had never imagined that crowds could be so pressing and he was amazed that they made any progress at all. At first he was quite frightened by all the noise and the people. Fear mixed with excitement left him in a daze.

'Don't worry,' said his father, seeing his expression. 'Everyone feels that way when they first arrive in India.'

Their Sikh driver kept his hand on the horn, but so did everyone else and this, with the tinkling of a million bicycle bells and the shouts and hoots which seemed to come from all sides, made it impossible to guess where the next danger was coming from. And yet, Jake gradually realized, it all seemed to work in an extraordinary, chaotic way. What was more, he noticed, almost everyone seemed cheerful, laughing and shouting at each other as they diced with death.

As they worked their way through the crowds which swarmed all over the road they were following, Jake could see that the canal alongside them was not the pretty waterway it had looked from the air. The water was filthy and full of litter. Terrible, unfamiliar smells wafted from it into the open windows of their taxi. And yet, people were bathing in the canal, washing themselves and their clothes in the brown muddy water. Their clothes were of the brightest colours Jake had ever seen: orange, purple, scarlet and azure. The people too, were beautiful: brown skinned with long black hair and flashing teeth.

'I think I'm going to like India,' he said to his father, who smiled and said, 'Well, it is a bit different from home.'

As the taxi wound its way through crowded back streets trying to find Bob's address, Jake wondered if he really wanted to stay in a school; but the moment they arrived he felt completely at home. It was a ramshackle series of buildings joined together by narrow passages which led to open play areas. Everyone was busy cooking or washing clothes and there was an atmosphere of happy bustle.

Bob met them in the courtyard where the taxi unloaded their bags and he helped them carry everything to their room.

'Can't stop now. I'm in the middle of a class,' he said. 'I'll show you round later.'

Jake liked him at once and, for the first time since arriving in India, he felt absolutely safe. Bob had that effect on people.

Their room was bare of furniture except for two beds made out of a wooden frame and string. Their room had a stone balcony, its yellow plaster falling off, which looked out over rooftops and back yards where people washed, cooked or slept. There was a palm tree in the garden with some strange nuts on top which were being eaten by a flock of green parakeets.

Jake had practically no luggage: just a couple of changes of clothes, a notebook in which his mother had made him promise he would keep a diary of everything he did, a small torch she had given him as a present and his trusty Swiss Army knife.

There were fifty boys and five girls in the school. They had all been rescued from the railway station and the streets of Calcutta by Bob and his team. When Jake and his father were shown around, their first impression was of how polite the children were. These were very tough children who had lived rough in a dangerous world and yet they had beautiful manners. A few sat quietly and looked away, but most were eager to crowd around Jake and ask him questions about England.

'Where do you go to school?'

'Have you a family?'

'Are you able to read and write?'

They seemed, and in class often were, model children, too good to be true. It was when Jake sat and chatted with them in the evening that he began to realize what an extraordinary thing Bob was doing. Having lived briefly with street children in Brazil, he found it easy to be natural with children from a completely different background to his own. He understood at once that their whole lives had revolved around crime and living rough because there had been nothing else. They had never had any other choice but to be outside the law. Bob's children had been given the idea by him that there might be another way than the life they were leading in the gutter and some of them were grasping the chance with both hands.

Others could not cope. There was nothing to stop anyone running away from the school, and quite often they did. Bob would usually try to track them down, and offer them the chance of coming back, trying to explain what their lives would hold. Sometimes he succeeded; sometimes he failed. It was a huge and impossible job he had set himself but the really extraordinary thing about it, Jake realized from talking to the children, was that they understood and welcomed the idea that it might just be possible to escape from the terrible poverty and degradations of life at the bottom of Indian society. They encouraged each other to try. It had been ten years since Bob had left the bank and already some of his children had passed through his school and, with his help, found good jobs with a promising future. More important to them even than this was that they had a family.

4
Calcutta

Jake's first day in Calcutta was very busy. It was hot and incredibly crowded but they managed to get a lot done. First, Peter Travis had to sort out his lecture programme at the Institute where he would be working. This was very boring for Jake as he had to sit for ages in dusty corridors while meetings were held behind closed doors.

'I'm sorry you're having such a dull time,' said his father, feeling bad when at last he was finished. 'What would you like to do now?'

Expecting a request for ice cream and some fun, he was surprised when Jake replied, 'I'd like to go to the tea company's offices now and see if they've heard from their head office about me visiting Granny's old tea plantation.'

'You are really keen to go there, aren't you?'

'I'd love to see where Granny Maisy lived. She's told me such a lot about it and it does sound a great place.' He had decided that it would be better not to tell his parents about the treasure as he was sure that they would stop him going if they thought he had an ulterior motive.

'OK,' replied his father, 'you have been very patient. Let's go now and see if they're still open.'

The tea company's offices were very smart, quite different from the university buildings they had spent the day in. Tea is a very important product in India, one of the country's main exports. The manager was extremely friendly and said he had been told by head office to give Jake every possible help.

'You grandfather was quite a legend and there are several company employees alive who remember him well. Now, the manager at Dangma knows you are coming, so it is simply a question of how soon you would like to go and for how long?'

'Well,' said Jake, glancing at his father. 'What I'd really like would be to spend as much time as possible at Dangma plantation. My father is going to be here at the Institute for a month and I don't want to be under his feet as he will be very busy.'

'When did you ever worry about being under my feet?' asked his father with a laugh.

The manager looked in a book which listed the company's employees and their families. Half to himself, he said 'Yes, Dangma. Let me see. The manager there is Mr Barua and he has a son, Dilip, of exactly your age. I know they will be happy to have you to stay for as long as you like. I will send a message right away and let you know tomorrow. Then I will make all the arrangements for your travel straight away. There will be no cost to you. Your grandfather was a great man and it will be our pleasure.'

Jake could hardly believe his ears. He had been worrying about how they were going to pay for him to fly up to Assam as he knew his father was on a tight budget. Mr Travis was clearly surprised, too. 'That's extremely kind of you,' he said. 'We're very grateful and I'm sure my son will have a fascinating time. I rather wish I could come too but I have a lot of work to do here.' Then they pored over maps of north-east India and the manager pointed out how the nearest airport to Dangma was at a place called Dibrugarh where, if all went well, Jake would be met and driven to the tea estate.

That evening, Jake asked Bob lots of questions about the school. This was partly because he was genuinely interested in how it all worked, and partly to stop his father asking about what he planned to do while he was at Dangma. He was afraid that if he was grilled he might have to let on about the treasure.

'How do you find the boys and girls who come here?' he asked. 'How do you know they'll like and it and how do you persuade them to try?'

'I don't,' said Bob. 'Each time I don't know if

it will work and I never persuade them. It's their choice and they're always free to change their minds. There are literally thousands of children at Howrah railway station and in the streets. Lots of them cope quite well. They are extraordinarily clever at finding ways of scraping a living, even though the people around them are mostly on the breadline themselves. I do look out for the ones who aren't coping and I do sometimes offer them the chance to try life here and see if they like it.'

'But how do you choose?' insisted Jake.

'The choice is usually made for me. We actually have more children than we can cope with already and I can't afford to expand, much as I would like to. But now that the school is known about, people will sometimes tell me about a child who is in a bad way and will die soon if something isn't done. Then I have to see if I can help. Sometimes it works; sometimes it doesn't. Then there are one or two who have gone back but who I know from the time they were here could make it if they tried again. I have to offer them another chance.'

'When do you do this?' asked Jake again.

'Always very late at night,' answered Bob. 'In the daytime they are all out begging or thieving and there's too much hustle and bustle; but at night it's quiet and they're mostly sleeping.'

'Isn't is dangerous?'

'It was at first. Some of the police thought I was there to do the children harm and they beat me up because of it. Also, there are some very tough customers about at night. But they mostly know me now and I'm pretty safe. I speak Hindi and Bengali, the two main languages around here, and I can talk myself out of most situations.'

'I'd love to come with you,' said Jake. 'Can I please?'

'Well, I never normally take anyone, new adults can be very threatening,' replied Bob doubtfully. 'But, as you're nearer their age . . . In fact, I was going out tonight and it would be interesting to see what they made of an English boy. You certainly seemed to get on well with them all here today and yesterday, but I don't suppose your father will like the idea.'

Jake looked imploringly at his father, who said, 'No chance, it sound far too dangerous. Anyway, I'm whacked and you must be, too. What time do you go out, Bob?'

'Between one and three in the morning.'

'Really, Jake, you wouldn't even wake up for it!'

'Oh please, Dad. I'd really like to go and I'm sure I'll be all right with Bob.'

'Well, as I've known Bob for years and I do trust him more than anyone else I know. . . There's certainly no one else I'd let you go out at

25

night in Calcutta with. If he agrees to take you, then I suppose it's OK by me, but I'd much rather you didn't go and if you *do* you must do exactly what he tells you. Go to bed now and I'll bet you won't want to wake up at one o'clock.' Turning to Bob he said quietly, 'He's sure to say he's too tired when the time comes but at least no one can say I'm not an indulgent father!'

But Jake did wake up and, slipping his Swiss Army knife into his pocket, he was ready in a moment, having gone to bed in his clothes. They drove in Bob's Jeep with an Indian teacher called Ravik through streets which were surprisingly full of people, even in the middle of the night.

When they reached the big railway station, parked and started walking, it was the smell that first struck Jake. The market next to the station had not yet been cleared up and the remains of the produce sold during the day lay all over the street. There were squashed tropical fruit of all sorts: mangoes, pineapples, bananas and lots more which Jake could not recognize. Everything smelled sweet and sickly. Then there was the meat market where blood still flowed in the gutters and the stench was of rotting flesh. The spice market was a shock. The unfamiliar scents were so strong that Jake had to hold his hand over his nose and eyes to protect them from the pungent aromas. They hurried past and entered the vast station building. Here there was an even worse smell.

As his eyes grew accustomed to the gloom, Jake could see the platforms with the railway lines between them, stretching out of the dimly lit building into the blackness of the night. There seemed to be bundles of clothing laid in rows everywhere he looked and it took him a moment to realize that each bundle contained a body. Mostly they were wrapped in grubby white sheets and lay so still that they looked like rows and rows of corpses. Then one would stir and roll over. Jake could not begin to count how many there were, but Bob and Ravik seemed to know their way around and, speaking quietly, began to explain the set-up as they walked through the station, carefully stepping over and around the bodies.

'Most of these are adult men and women who have nowhere else to go at night. At least it's under cover here and there are some taps for washing under.'

'Are they allowed to use the public lavatories?' asked Jake.

'Not really. You have to pay and most of them have no money. They use the railway lines.' Jake now realized what the new stench assailing his nostrils was.

'Of course, there are lots of genuine travellers here, too. People who have missed their train or

27

who are making an early start and want to be sure of a place. The trains here in India are very crowded.

'Different groups sleeping here tend to stick together. Over there are the deaf and mute. They have a hard time as beggars but they are always friendly.' As they walked past, several of the bundles sat up and Jake could see flashing eyes and teeth as they smiled and waved at Bob.

'Over there are mostly lepers, and the limbless beggars are nearby. They are no trouble, but the men in that area are best avoided. Some of the more violent and unpleasant characters are over there, so I think we'll head this way. They can be pretty aggressive to stick close to me. We need to be careful and to know what to do if it gets nasty.'

Jake looked nervously at the rows of bundles. He felt self-conscious in his clean, new trainers and relatively smart clothes amongst such ragged poverty. 'But where are the children?' he asked. 'And how do they get here?'

'They're scattered about,' answered Bob. 'There's a group over there.' He pointed at a cluster of smaller bundles. 'Those are OK. They've got each other.'

'It's a sad story how they get here,' Ravik took up the explanation. 'It's all due, really, to my country's terrible population problem. India is the second biggest country in the world, after

China, with a population of over 700 million and growing fast. Lots of children get orphaned or have to leave home because there simply isn't enough food to go round. Sometimes only one of their parents dies but they get lost or thrown out. Some of them are as young as four or five but somehow they get to hear about Howrah Station and they stow away on trains and come here from all over India. There seems to be a myth that the streets of Calcutta are paved with gold and so they come in their thousands. Sadly, it is not like they expect at all when they arrive. All they can do is beg and get into all sorts of trouble as well as suffering awful diseases. Most die young.'

At that moment, a ragged boy of about ten scrambled to his feet, threw down his bundle of rags and ran over to Bob. He grasped his hand and grinned up into his face. Then chattered away, pointing across the station and making funny faces.

'This is Amrit,' said Bob after a while. 'He's a great character. A dreadful rogue, but a good friend of mine. He has no desire to come to the school as he makes out very well on his own, but he worries about the little ones. He has just told me that there's a small boy in trouble over there. We'd better go and have a look.'

Amrit let go of Bob's hand, stuck his tongue out at Jake, flashed him a wicked smile and dashed behind a pillar. They walked on. Jake saw a small bundle lying by itself and went over to look at it. A small boy wrapped in a thin sheet lay on some sacking. 'He's all by himself,' he said to Bob, who had explained that it was the ones who had no friends who were the least able to look after themselves.

'No. *He's* doing all right,' said Bob. 'Look. He's got three sacks under him. Any boy with three sacks has got some scam going and is probably surviving quite well. It's the little lonely ones who don't know what to do that starve, or get sold as slaves.'

They found Sanjit huddled at the base of a pillar. He was very small, seemed about six years old, had nothing to cover himself and he was shivering and crying. Bob bent down and spoke quietly to him. He shook his head violently at first and tried to run away, but Bob pointed to Jake and said something which made Sanjit pause. 'I've told him you're an English boy and that you want to help him. Do you mind giving him one of your sweets?'

Jake took a sweet out of his pocket. Sanjit snatched it from him and stuffed it into his mouth, his eyes wide with fright. He still seemed ready to run, shaking his head whenever Bob said anything. Then, just as Jake thought that they were about to give up and walk away, Amrit appeared. He cuffed the little boy cheerfully and chattered away to him in Bengali. The small boy listened, looking doubtfully at Bob. Then, abruptly, he nodded and held out his hand to Jake for another sweet, which he was given. Again he grabbed it hungrily.

Accompanied by Amrit, who kept talking to the smaller boy the whole time, they all made their way back to the Jeep and got in. It took a bit of persuading the get Sanjit in but at last he climbed in by himself and sat stiffly in the back. As they drove away, Jake looked back to see the solitary figure of Amrit standing under a street light, waving cheerfully. 'How can he be so cheerful?' he asked.

'He's got it made in his book,' said Bob. 'It's all he's ever known and he's good at it. It's sad because he'll certainly die young, probably after getting ill. But he sees himself as a success and that's what matters, I suppose. He's a very good thief, is Amrit, luckily for him. He's a very good-hearted boy. I like him.'

When they reached the school Sanjit was, much to his fury, given a bath, scrubbed and disinfected, before being put in a dormitory with ten other small boys. During the next day, for much of which Jake slept, Sanjit sat by himself, refusing to speak to anyone and staring furiously at those who approached him.

'Give him time,' said Bob.

5
Dangma

Early the following morning, Jake was fetched in a taxi by an employee of the tea company, who took him to the airport.

'You *will* behave yourself, won't you?' asked his father anxiously as he said goodbye. 'I don't think your mother will every forgive me if you get into any trouble.'

'Don't worry, Dad,' shouted Jake out of the taxi window. 'I'm just going to learn about tea and about what Granny Maisy and Grandfather Beckett did.' He gave a faint grin and told himself that he would do his best not to get into trouble.

As the plane came in to land at Dibrugarh, it swooped over a huge river. This, Jake knew from studying a map his father had given him, was the Brahmaputra, one of the world's most important rivers. It rises in Tibet, far to the west of Dibrugarh, turns sharply south to cut by deep gorges through the Himalayas, the only river to do so, and then runs back as far again to the west before flowing south once more through Bangladesh to the sea. Its name means Son of Brahma, the Hindu creator-god. The river fertilizes the rich plains it runs through with silt brought down from the mountains, and steamers can navigate up it as far as Dibrugarh, 800 miles from the sea. Jake could see wide sandbanks which looked like big seaside beaches and little desert islands with trees growing on them. It was not at all the sort of landscape he had been expecting.

He was pushed and jostled by the crowd in the terminal building and for a moment felt quite lost and alone. Then he saw a big sign held above the heads of all the people with JAKE written on it and he struggled over to it. A small Indian wearing a huge blue turban above a massive 'handlebar' moustache and beard dropped the sign to the ground when he saw Jake and hurried over to grasp his right hand in both of his.

'Oh Mr Jake!' he said breathlessly, 'I have been so worried that you might be lost. You see, I am responsible for your health and welfare and it is more than my job is worth to fall down on it. I am truly honoured and delighted to meet you and I am utterly at your convenience.'

Jake was a bit overwhelmed by this welcome, but it did make him feel very important and so he drew himself up and said, in as grown-up a voice as he could manage, 'I'm very pleased to meet you. What is your name, please?'

'Oh yes, indeed,' answered the other. 'My name is Singh, I am a Sikh, you see, and I hope that we are going to become the very firmest of friends.' Singh's eyes twinkled behind his beard and Jake, for the first of many times, found that it was difficult not to smile when in his company.

They hurried out to a smart Land Rover with the tea company's logo on it. Singh talked non-stop for the whole of the two-hour drive to Dangma. 'My life is all to do with happiness. What else is there? I like to make everybody happy wherever I am and, you know, it is the same with all my family. We are Sikhs, did you not know that? That is why we wear this turban. I have to fold it very carefully and put it on every day. It is the same for all my brothers. I have very many brothers and some sisters also.'

Jake had never met anyone who talked so much as was beginning to hope he would not have to spend the whole of his time with him, when he began to talk about Dangma.

'Oh yes. You will love it very much there. It is a most splendid place, a relic of your British Raj, I think. The bungalow is big, very big indeed and Mr Barua, who is my boss, is a very important man. Five thousand people he has working for him which means, I think, that he is very clever. This, however, I am not able to say about his son, Dilip. Now there is a boy who is very much trouble. I see that you are not like him and I hope that you will listen to Singh and not to young Dilip. He and I have many times been close to fisticuffs.'

Jake was not sure how serious Singh was being but he began to look forward to meeting Dilip.

The country had been changing for some time as the road approached a range of hills rising steeply out of the plain. Everything was much greener. They passed through some patches of dense forest where huge trees towered over them and other areas where neat rows of trimmed bushes stretched away into the distance. 'What are those bushes?' Jake asked.

'Oh my goodness! Do you not know tea bushes when you see them? These are where the tea leaves grow which you drink back home I am sure. But these are of the inferior sort. Wait until you see the ones at Dangma. They are the very best.' And Singh puffed his chest out with pride as though he was personally responsible. It really was impossible not to smile in his company.

When, at last, they drove through what seemed like miles of the neatest bushes yet and along a good straight estate road up towards Dangma itself, Jake was impressed. The bungalow stood on a low hill above the plantation. The roof was green, just as Granny Maisy had described it, and it was surrounded by a magnificent garden full of brightly coloured flowers. There were several fine trees, some with brilliant orange flowers all over them, and one magnificent specimen on the lawn from which creepers hung down to the ground. Two small cannons guarded the entrance gate and, as they swept through, Singh tooted the horn loudly to announce their arrival.

The bungalow did not seem to have a front door. Instead, they pulled up at a short flight of steps leading up to a wide open veranda with tables and comfortable chairs spread about. A grey-haired man and a stout lady in a sari were sitting together on a sofa, drinking tea. As they rose to meet him, two white-coated servants rushed out, opened all the doors of the Land Rover and started a small fight over who should carry Jake's single canvas bag. Clearly they had been expecting such an important guest to have lots of luggage. In the end they took a handle each and carried it off into the house.

Jake walked up the steps to meet the couple.

'My dear Jake,' said the grey-haired man. 'It is a real pleasure to have you here. I am Mr Barua and this is my wife Mrs Barua. I'm afraid our son, Dilip, has disappeared for the moment. Will you have a cup of tea?' In spite of the strange surroundings, Jake felt immediately at home. Mr and Mrs Barua were so welcoming and left him in no doubt that they really were pleased to have him stay for as long as he liked.

'I'm afraid it is sometimes a bit lonely for Dilip here,' said Mrs Barua. 'He is a good boy but he does get up to a lot of mischief. I am sure you are going to be a good influence on him.'

'Whoops!' thought Jake.

'Now you must want to see your room and have a rest,' Mrs Barua stated after Jake had drunk his tea. 'You must be tired after your journey.' Jake was not at all tired, but he thought he had better do as was expected and so said nothing. He was shown to a very comfortable room with a bathroom leading off it. It had a high ceiling with wooden rafters and a cool tiled floor.

'Dilip's room is through here,' explained Mr Barua opening a door. 'You can be private or you can have the door open when it will be like a dormitory if you like. I suggest you have a rest now before supper.'

Jake unpacked his few possessions from the bag which had been put in his room, lay down on the bed and took a deep breath. I've done it! he thought. Even if I don't find the treasure, I've made it to Granny Maisy's old home and I never really thought I would. He let his breath out slowly, closed his eyes and dropped off to sleep.

6
Dilip

Jake awoke to feel something tickling his chest. For a moment, he couldn't remember where he was – and then it all came rushing back. He was in India, the tropics, where all sorts of nasty creepy crawlies lived. Lying still and with his eyes closed, he began to imagine all the scenes he had watched in films when horrible, poisonous creatures had dropped on to the hero. Surely it wasn't happening to him.

Cautiously, he opened one eye and peered out between his half closed lids. There was something on his chest and it was moving. Scarcely believing what he was seeing he realized that it really was an enormous spider, by far the biggest he had ever seen. There was something wrong, however. Spiders he had met before wiggled their legs. This one just bounced up and down, almost as though its thread, from which it was hanging, was elastic. Now that he looked closely, but still without moving or opening his eyes any wider, he could see that the spider's eyes were dull, like paint and its body seemed to be made of rubber. He decided to turn the tables on who- ever was playing a trick on him, and he had a strong suspicion who that was.

Moving very slowly, he stretched one arm out towards the bedside table where he had left his knife. His hand felt it, picked it up and reached behind his head to meet the other hand, so that he could open one of the blades. All this time the spider stayed where it was, though it began to bounce up and down more actively. Once the blade was open, Jake calmly reached forward with both hands above the spider, took its thread in one hand and cut it with the knife. Holding the thread, from which the toy spider now dan- gled limply, he got up and started to walk towards the bathroom. Halfway there he stopped, turned and looked up at the rafters. 'Do you want your spider back, Dilip, or shall I flush it away?'

There was a peal of laughter from the ceiling and a grinning Indian boy swung himself down on to the bed. 'Well done, Jake!' he said. 'You win that one hands down. I might have known I wouldn't be able to frighten someone who has been to the Amazon!'

'Don't ever try anything like that again, Dilip,' said Jake, trying to look cross. Then he, too, grinned. 'I think I'm going to like it here,' he said.

'I'm sorry,' said Dilip, 'only everyone's been going on about how clever and brave you are and how I must be nice to you, that I just wanted to give you a fright. But now you've turned the tables on me and shown you really are brave.'

'Don't you believe it!' laughed Jake. 'I'm terrified of spiders, and I would have been petrified if that had been a real spider. Only, luckily for me, I spotted it was a fake right away and realized it must be you on the other end of the string. And I'm really not clever and brave. I'm completely out of my depth here and I know nothing about India so I'm going to need your help to see me through.'

'That's OK then,' said Dilip, cheerfully. 'I know everything and tomorrow I'll show you round. Only now we'd better go and have supper. I'm in enough trouble already for not being there when you arrived. If you tell them what I did I'll probably be sent to bed without any.' And he looked at Jake enquiringly.

'Your secret is safe with me – unless you try any more tricks,' answered Jake. 'But it looks to me as though you get away with murder already. Singh's been telling me about you.'

'That man's awful!' exclaimed Dilip. 'You don't want to believe anything he says, especially about me.'

'I think he's funny,' said Jake.

'Funny!' shrieked Dilip. 'The man's a pain!'

'I think that's just because you can't get round him like you seem to manage with everyone else,' said Jake and Dilip grinned again, a bit sheepishly.

Supper was tricky for Jake as some of the food was strange and, while he was trying to impress the Baruas with his good manners and do things right, Dilip was ready to tease him at every opportunity. Jake also found the quiet white-coated servants, who flitted about whisking away plates before he had finished and placing new and unfamiliar dishes in front of him, very distracting. The men looked so serious.

The food was familiar: meat, rice and vegetables. Jake had been worried, though he had not mentioned it to his parents, that he would have to eat nothing but curry, which he ate at home now and again but which was not his favourite food.

'You see,' said Mrs Barua, 'we are having a meal just like you eat at home.'

And Jake replied, 'Yes. It's delicious,' before he had taken any. It was, too, only there were unexpected dangers lurking.

When he took a spoonful of what he thought was just another green vegetable from a bowl beside his place and put it in his mouth, he thought it was going to blow his head off. It was some kind of spice that he realized you were only meant to take a pinch of. He was aware

that Dilip was having a laughing fit into his nap-
kin as he reached for his glass of water to
quench the fire. Fortunately, the Baruas were
talking to each other and didn't notice. After
that he was more careful, testing each dish
before eating it and, gradually, he found that he
liked the different tastes.

'Tomorrow, I think you would like to see
around Dangma,' said Mr Barua. 'Un-
fortunately, I am very busy at the moment as we
are in the middle of the tea harvest, but I will get
Singh to take you around and Dilip will tell you
all about how tea is produced.'

'Thank you very much,' said Jake. He was
itching to start looking for treasure but he realized that he was genuinely interested in how tea
was made.

'Good, then I suggest we have an early night.
You must be tired and we get up at dawn here.
That is at 6 o'clock. Dilip! I do not want any
noise from your rooms tonight. Do you understand?'

Although Mr Barua was speaking sternly to
his son, Jake had the feeling that the remark
was addressed to both of them and so he
replied, 'Yes,' in unison with Dilip. They were
allowed to go to their rooms then and, though
Dilip wanted to play a game, Jake suddenly did
feel terribly tired and begged to be allowed to
sleep.

'I will show you everything tomorrow,' were the last words he heard through the open door between their rooms as he closed his eyes.

7
Tea

Breakfast on the veranda was both beautiful and delicious with the result that Jake started the day feeling great. For a start, it was cool in the dawn with the mist lying over the plantation below them and only the tops of the many trees, which grew between the tea bushes to shade them, showing above the grey blanket. They were in sunshine and the garden was full of birds which sang and flew about as though they were in a zoo. 'Why are there so many birds?' Jake asked.

'Because of all my lovely flowers,' answered Mrs Barua, looking pleased.

They ate wonderful fruit, many types of which Jake had never tasted before. There were melons and pawpaws, grapefruit and mangoes, already peeled and stuck on a fork, ready to eat. There were also pineapples and pomegranates, and all so sweet, succulent and juicy that he hardly knew what to eat first.

'You see,' said Mr Barua, when Jake commented on this, 'here we eat fruit when they are ripe. But you have to eat ones which have been sent across the world unripe, so as to survive the journey. They are never the same, I find, when I am in London.'

'Do you go there often?' asked Jake.

'Oh yes. Tea is very big business and we still sell most of ours to the UK.'

Just how big a business, Jake was to learn when they started going around the plantation. They seemed to drive for miles along estate roads between incredibly neat rows of tea bushes.

'How are the bushes kept so regular?' asked Jake. 'Do they use a hedge trimmer?'

'Oh my goodness no. What a funny idea!' laughed Singh, who was driving. 'No, no! All that neatness, it comes only from the fingers of the many ladies who pluck off the leaves to make the tea. It is always ladies who do the plucking because they have more delicate fingers, don't you see? Ha, ha,' and Singh rolled about laughing in the front seat.

Dilip was not pleased to see his new friend being laughed at, although Jake didn't mind a bit. Singh always seemed completely well intentioned to him. 'You will shut up and leave the talking to me!' he said rudely to the driver. 'I am the one who is showing Jake around here.'

Singh had a funny way of waggling his head, which reminded Jake of a small china Buddha

Granny Maisy had in her room. He did this when he was laughing, but also when he was angry and Jake could see that his head was positively lurching from side to side as he restrained himself from quarrelling with the boss's son.

To change the subject, Jake asked, 'What are those buildings over there?' and he pointed at some large sheds ahead with chimneys coming out of them.

'Those are the factory buildings,' Dilip replied, 'and that's where we're going.'

When they drove in through the gates it was like entering a beehive. There were people everywhere, pushing great trolleys about and scraping up the dirt. Inside, from where a loud buzzing emerged, there were many more people working in rows, sifting tea on endless moving belts which carried the leaves past them. There were great vats from which steam rose and everywhere there was the hum of machinery and voices. Jake didn't really understand all the things Dilip was telling him above the noise but he was impressed by the activity and by how clean everything was.

'It must be clean,' Dilip said proudly. 'After all you are going to drink it one day.'

'I don't much like tea, actually,' admitted Jake, and Dilip punched him as they suddenly dashed together round a corner. Singh had been following them closely and listening disapprovingly to

Dilip's explanations. Clearly he was longing to give his version.

'Let's lose him,' said Dilip as they ran. 'I know a good place.'

'Are you sure we should?' asked Jake. He felt bad about escaping, but Singh had stopped to gossip with one of the foremen. He seemed to know everyone and could never resist a chat. By the time he looked up the boys had vanished and he spent the next couple of hours fruitlessly searching for them, and becoming crosser and crosser.

Meanwhile, Jake and Dilip had slipped out of the factory buildings by a secret gap in the wall. They scrambled down a steep bank to a stream which ran through the plantation.

'There are some turtles here which you can catch if you are clever,' said Dilip. So they had a good time trying without much success to creep up on the turtles, which they could see apparently sound asleep on logs in the sun. But they always plopped off into the water the moment one of the boys came too close.

At last they decided they had better go back to Singh, only to realize that they were now covered in mud and soaking wet from the number of near misses they had had.

'Oh dear,' said Jake. 'I think we're going to be in trouble. What would we have done with a turtle anyway if we'd caught one?'

'Well, I thought if we caught two we might have a race.'

'You're crazy,' said Jake, 'but I admit it's been fun. Let's go and face the music.'

Singh was hopping from one foot to the other with rage when they found him. 'I will tell! I will tell!' he kept repeating. 'This is too much. Too much!'

'No you won't,' replied Dilip calmly, 'because if you do I'll say you went off gossiping and we got lost and were very frightened.'

Looking from one to the other, Jake could tell that this was an old argument, one that Dilip would win, and he felt sorry for Singh, who was clearly no match for the spoiled and indulged son of the boss. He thought he had better not interfere and so went along with the story they concocted about how the Jeep had got stuck in a pond and they had had to help push it out, and so had become covered in mud. This story the Baruas believed, and they were sent off to wash and change their clothes before lunch. There was a lot of clucking and fussing from Mrs Barua.

Over lunch, Mr Barua told Jake more about tea. 'Now you have been over our plantation and factory, you will begin to understand what a big operation we have here. We look after the tea plants very carefully. Each one is weeded and pruned all the time and when it comes to

48

harvesting the crop we pluck the leaves gently by hand. Then you saw how much work goes into selecting the different qualities, grading the leaves and drying them exactly right. It is a big business and it is my life. Did they tell you that some of our tea bushes are as much as fifty years old?'

'Really?' exclaimed Jake. 'That means some of them were planted by my grandfather.'

Jake could see that Mr Barua was very proud of Dangma and would happily have talked about it for hours; but he had to get back to his office and Jake had his first chance to explore the garden. It was full of potential hiding places, but few that looked as though they would have remained hidden for fifty years. Unless, of course, the treasure had been buried. But, if so, where to begin looking? After all, he couldn't very well start digging holes all over the place without arousing suspicions.

For a long time Jake just stood on the veranda looking across the garden and trying to imagine where a frightened young mother-to-be in a hurry might have hidden a small tin box. He wished Granny Maisy had given him a clue but all she had said was, 'In the garden . . . In . . .' In what? In a hole in the ground, perhaps.

'Why are you looking like that?' He realized Dilip, who had said he was going to his room, must have been watching him for some time. He also decided that he stood very little chance of finding the treasure on his own and that he had better share his secret with Dilip.

'You're not going to believe this,' he said at last. 'But I had a reason for coming here . . .' And he briefly told him about the tin box.

'Golly,' said Dilip, staring at Jake with eyes as wide as saucers. 'You really are old Mr Beckett's grandson! Everyone still talks about what a hero he was. Now you are going to be one too.'

'We haven't found anything yet,' said Jake, trying to calm down the other boy, who was leaping about with excitement. 'And we won't if you tell anyone about this. It's a secret between us. And if we do find the treasure, you'll be a hero, too.' This had the effect of making Dilip stop hopping and become very serious.

'You can rely on me,' he promised. 'I won't tell a soul. Not even Rajah.'

'Who is Rajah?' asked Jake.

'He is my elephant,' answered Dilip, and it was Jake's turn to be impressed.

'You haven't got an elephant!' he said.

'Yes I have indeed,' retorted Dilip crossly. 'He's not very big yet, but I'm teaching him and one day he is going to be a mighty beast.'

'Wow!' said Jake. 'Can I meet him?'

'Of course, but not today. He's kept a few miles from here in the foothills and we will need

Singh to drive us there. I think we had better wait a bit before asking him.'

Jake agreed. 'Where do you think Granny Maisy might have hidden it?' he asked.

'What about in the pond?'

At the end of the garden, at the foot of the mound on which the bungalow was built, a pond had been excavated and some rare ducks were being bred there. It had a small island on it, reached by a plank bridge, where there was a little wooden house. That looked like a good place. The boys made a careful crossing to step on to the slippery mud of the island. Inside the house were nesting boxes for the ducks and they felt in each one. They found some eggs and, in one, an angry duck which pecked at Jake's hand. There were no cracks or other hiding places in the roof and they crossed back over the plank feeling dejected.

'This isn't going to be easy,' muttered Jake. 'That pond probably wasn't there in the war anyway.'

'I know!' shouted Dilip suddenly. 'The cannon – they've been here since the war. They were captured from the Japanese. That's where I'd hide something.'

They raced round the hill to the front entrance and skidded to a stop beside the first cannon.

'Go on! Feel inside the barrel,' urged Dilip.

Jake hesitated. Having just been pecked by a duck, he didn't feel like groping inside somewhere he couldn't see.

'You do it,' he suggested.

'No. It's your treasure,' said Dilip. In the end they got a stick and used it to poke out lots of debris from the barrel. There were old cigarette packets and sweet papers, bottle tops and bones, but no tin box. After a lot of scraping they could see the stick through the touch hole and they knew that the barrel was empty. The other barrel was worse as, in addition to all the usual debris, some stinging ants had made a nest there. The first Jake knew of this was after he had been poking around for a while with his stick, hoicking out rubbish. Suddenly he felt a burning sensation on his back, rapidly followed by another on his side and several on his shoulders.

'What's happening?' he shouted as he frantically tried to put his hands over all the sore places at once.

'Looks like you've got ants in your pants,' said Dilip laughing. 'You'd better take your shirt off.'

Sure enough, when Jake wrenched his shirt over his head, tearing it in the process, he found that he had lots of little red ants running over his body. He and Dilip slapped at them until they were all gone, Dilip slapped rather harder than necessary, Jake thought.

'Come into the house and we'll put some ointment on the bites,' said Dilip, trying to look sym-
pathetic. 'It's not serious. It's happened to me
lots of times. My mother has just the thing for
it.'

Mrs Barua's ointment soothed the bites as
Dilip had promised and Jake was sent to lie
down. When Mr Barua came back after work,
they asked if they could fire the cannons, just to
be sure there was nothing still in them.
'Certainly not!' said Mr Barua. 'They would
probably blow up. It was your grandfather who
captured them, but they were not brought here
until some time after the war was over.'

The boys looked at each other. 'When was the
duck pond made?' asked Dilip.

'Oh, only a few years ago, just before you were
born,' said Mr Barua.

Jake muttered, 'Back to the drawing board,'
under his breath.

As it was getting dark, there was no more time
to search other parts of the garden. But Mr
Barua had another idea anyway. He said,
'Tonight there is a festival in the village where
most of our workers live. Would you like to go,
Jake? I think you would find it interesting.'

'Yes, please,' said Jake. If he couldn't be treasure hunting tonight he might as well, he
thought gloomily.

'It will be fun,' said Dilip encouragingly, seeing his mood. And it was. There were dancers singing and swaying to the rhythm of a drum in a long line. Stalls had been set up selling all sorts of trinkets. Jake found a pretty bead necklace to take home as a present for his mother and an old English teacup with a flower pattern for Granny Maisy. It was very cheap and cracked, but he thought it would remind her of India.

A crowd had gathered around someone sitting on the ground. The boys squeezed through to see what was going on. A very old man with long white straggly hair, and wearing nothing but a white *dhoti* – a loincloth– was sitting cross-legged on a mat. A pile of small stones and a woven basket were at his side. In front crouched a young woman in a sari, the cloth held in front of her face, over which stared two frightened eyes. The old man's hand lay on the top of her head and he was mumbling rapidly. His voice rose and he said a few clear words. The girl stumbled to her feet and ran back into the crowd, her head held down and buried in her sari.

'What was all that about?' asked Jake.

'He said she would have a baby and it would be a boy,' translated Dilip. 'Now she will be very pleased. That was what she wanted to hear.'

'How does he know?' asked Jake.

'Oh he is a "jadugar" – a magician – and a very wise man. He knows everything.'

'Well, I suppose he has a fifty per cent chance of being right that time,' said Jake with a laugh. Then he noticed to his embarrassment that the old man was staring straight at him, almost as though he had heard and understood what he had said. Standing up, he tottered over to where the boys were squashed in the edge of the crowd and said something directly to Jake.

'He is asking if you would like proof that he knows things,' said Dilip. 'He says it will cost you nothing if you agree. You cannot refuse. It would be rude.'

Jake was reluctantly led to the mat and made to sit down. The crowd leaned inward eagerly. It was not every day they saw an English boy having his fortune told. Dilip sat beside Jake to interpret.

'He wants you to ask him a question,' said Dilip. 'Something he could not know.'

Jake thought for a moment, then said, 'Ask him the name of my dog.' At home on the farm Jake had a West Highland terrier called Saki with whom he played endlessly during the holidays, throwing balls and chasing rabbits in the woods. He had missing Saki since he had been in India.

The old man closed his eyes and started mumbling again. Jake thought of Saki. He could see him clearly in his mind's eye, surprisingly clearly, he thought. The old man was fumbling in the wicker basket. He brought out a ragged scrap of paper and a stub of a pencil. Very slowly and still with his eyes shut, he pressed the paper to the ground with one hand and started to write with the other.

Jake felt a cold shiver run up his spine as he watched the four letters of his dog's name slowly but unmistakably take shape on the paper. The old man's eyes snapped open and once again he looked straight at Jake. Respectfully, Jake nodded and bowed low to the ground. It seemed the right thing to do and the crowd clapped delightedly. Sitting up again and looking into those penetrating eyes once more, he said without turning his head, 'Can you ask him if he can find things?'

Dilip spoke, the old man replied and Dilip translated. 'He says he can but it takes time and will cost you 50 Rupees.'

'That's OK,' said Jake. 'That's nothing, barely £1.'

'It's a lot to him,' answered Dilip. 'He says you must go to his house tomorrow. And now we must go.'

They ran back to where Singh was waiting by the Jeep. 'We must tell no one about this,' said Dilip. 'I am quite frightened.'

'I agree,' said Jake.

8
Dreams

'Thank you for letting me see around yesterday, Mr Barua,' Jake said at breakfast the next day. 'I found it very interesting.'

'That's not exactly the way I heard it,' replied Dilip's father. 'You boys really must stop teasing Singh so much. He was most upset about the tricks you played on him.'

'Sorry, Daddy,' said Dilip, looking anything but. 'We won't do it again.'

'I doubt that,' Mr Barua tried unsuccessfully to look stern. 'But I wish you would try. He is a very loyal and good-hearted man.'

'May we go down to the village again, please?' asked Jake, seeing this was a good moment. 'I didn't get chance to look around properly with the crowds at the festival last night.'

'Yes, yes. But please try to be good, both of you,' was the reply.

To avoid having Singh hanging about and checking up on them, the boys rode down to the village on one of the estate tractors and trailers.

There were several workers, men and women, on board and it was fun bouncing along in the open air, hanging on to the sides. On the way they passed a group of three elephants with fierce-looking men riding them while others walked alongside. The elephants were painted with designs in red and black and Jake found it an astonishing and wonderful sight, the most romantic he had yet seen in India.

'Who are they?' he asked Dilip.

'Bad men, dangerous men. Do not look at them. They are loggers, they steal the big trees in the forest and make big money from the logs. Everyone is very frightened of them.'

Jake noticed that the chatter in the trailer stopped as they passed the elephants and took some time to start up again.

'My Rajah will be as big as the biggest of those elephants one day,' said Dilip. 'But I will never allow him to be used for bad things like those ones.'

Before Jake could ask more they arrived at the village and were dropped off. The old jadugar's house looked very poor and there was a strong smell from the open drain which flowed past it. Jake began to wonder if they were wise to have come and Dilip was looking nervous too.

'He is a very wise man, but they say he can cast spells. Are you sure you have to find this thing?'

'Yes, please Dilip. Help me to do that. I can't do this by myself and I really need you now. Let's see this through together.' Jake was now full of determination so Dilip took a deep breath and led the way into the house.

Inside it was dark. They were led by a small child into a bare room where Jake could just make out the old man sitting cross-legged in the middle on the earth floor. The only furniture was a wooden frame bed with woven criss-cross ropes to lie on.

The two boys squatted against a wall and Dilip spoke to the old man who answered at length.

'He says it will be difficult to find what you seek. He says he can only help you if you help him. It is something lost a long time ago and only you have the clues to finding it. Do you agree? Oh! And he says it is so difficult it will cost you 100 Rupees. I think he may be a naughty man trying to cheat you, but I have also been told that he is very wise.'

Jake agreed at once; 100 Rupees sounded like a lot, but in British money it was very little. It was worth it just to find out what he would do.

'Lie on the charpoy,' Dilip instructed.

'What's that?' asked Jake.

'That's what we call the bed over there,' explained Dilip and Jake dutifully went and lay on it. It was surprisingly comfortable.

'Now close your eyes and listen. I will not be saying any more. He is telling me to shut up,' and Dilip giggled nervously. He was beginning to wonder what he had let his new friend in for.

The old man began to chant. Jake listened to the gentle rhythm and began to feel sleepy. Images came into his mind like snapshots being flicked slowly through an album. First came Saki sitting up, keen and white, begging him to throw his ball. Then his mother in the garden picking flowers. She seemed to be listening to something, puzzled. Next there were a series of moments recalling people he had met during his Amazon adventures in Peru and Brazil: his Peruvian friend, Jaime; the Indians who had saved his life and looked after him when he was lost in the jungle; the beautiful children who smiled at him and held out their hands; Pedro, the boy with whom he had gone hunting with bows and arrows who nodded gravely at him, then grinned and made as though to draw his bow and shoot an arrow; the old shaman who blew smoke in his face; the black street boy, Orlando, with his shock of white hair; then the English girl, Lizzie, sitting up in bed. Each of them, like his mother, was looking up as though at something half heard.

For a moment he looked down on all the fond familiar faces of the people with whom he had spent such exciting and happy days the year before; then he was standing in the garden of the house where his grandmother lived. She was lying in her favourite deckchair with her eyes shut.

'Hello, Granny Maisy!' he said.

'Hello! Jake,' she replied, her eyes snapping open. 'My goodness, you gave me a start. I thought you were in India.'

'I am really, I think,' said Jake, 'only you never told me where the treasure is and I can't find it.'

For a moment his grandmother's eyes filled with tears and he thought he was going to lose her again, as he had so often before when he had brought up the subject. Then she looked directly at him and said, 'It's in the big tree in the garden of course, you silly boy. Couldn't you have guessed that on your own? It's in a hole up in the first fork. You'll have to climb. I thought it was the perfect hiding place.'

Instantly, before he could thank her, Jake was back on the charpoy. He had been there all the time, of course, but it felt as though he had landed from a great height. Jake reeled in surprise, and when he had regained his composure, said to Dilip, 'Will you thank him very much for me, please? Tell him he has led me to the answer to my question and I will pay him more than the 100 Rupees if he wants me to.'

'No. He wants no more,' Dilip passed on to Jake after talking to the old jadugar. And so they paid and left the little house. Jake was shaking as they came out on to the street and he had to sit down on a low wall to catch his breath. He felt as though he had been running for miles. Dilip looked at him curiously and asked, 'Are you going to tell me what you dreamt about? I could see your eyelids flickering and I know you were dreaming. Can you remember any of it?'

'Oh yes,' said Jake. 'I can remember it all. I think I have just had the most extraordinary experience of my life!' And on the long walk back to the bungalow he told his friend all about where he had been in his dreams; and that led on to telling him all about what had happened to him in South America. Only then did he tell him where the treasure was.

9
Snakes

'But you can never climb *that* tree,' exclaimed Dilip, his eyes wide with horror when Jake reached the climax of his story.

'Why ever not? It looks easy enough to me. You don't have to if it's too high for you.'

'No!' Dilip almost shouted. 'You don't understand. No one ever goes too near that tree. Two big cobras live in it. They are very, very dangerous and certainly will not let you pass them.'

'Oh dear,' said Jake thoughtfully. 'Then we'll just have to find a way.'

'Please give up the idea now, Jake,' pleaded Dilip. 'There are lots of other things we can do and I promise not to play any more tricks. But don't go near those snakes. They will kill you.'

'Don't worry, Dilip,' said Jake, surprised at how calm and sure he now felt. 'I have not come all this way to play games and I have a feeling that a lot of people want me to succeed.' He thought of all the friends he had just been with and it gave him a good feeling, as though they were standing beside him and urging him on.

'If you are determined to do this foolish thing, then you must speak with Ram Das,' said Dilip. 'He is the oldest servant here and he has lived in this house for many years. He knows about the snakes.'

They went into the back of the bungalow, going through the kitchen, where Dilip stole some cakes and was chased out by the big, laughing cook. Ram Das was a tiny, wizened man and he was sitting on a battered charpoy with his eyes shut.

'He does almost no work now, but he has been here for so long that my father says he is useful just because he knows everything,' whispered Dilip.

'Ask him about the snakes,' said Jake impatiently. To his surprise, Dilip approached the charpoy quietly and coughed gently. Ram Das opened his eyes and Dilip put his hands together in the polite Indian greeting called 'namaste' and bowed to him. This was so different from the way Dilip usually treated the other servants, which had rather shocked Jake, that he realized Ram Das must be someone special.

'He wants to know why you are asking about the snakes,' Dilip translated after he and Ram Das had spoken for a while.

'Tell him I am interested because there are no

cobras where I live and I want to know if they are dangerous.'

'Very dangerous, he says. Many people in this country die from snake bite and the cobra is the most poisonous.'

'Then why are these ones allowed to live in the garden?'

'Because they are holy,' Dilip translated. 'They guard the house. Also they keep away all rats and other snakes. They will never harm anyone as long as I, Ram Das, look after them. I understand them, I worship them, I feed them.'

'How do you feed them?'

'Every day I give them a little fresh milk. On holy days I give them some money also. I call them Naga and I say prayers to them.' And the little man began to chant in a high, reedy voice.

'What are the words?' asked Jake.

'I can't understand all of them because it is in a strange dialect. But it all about "Naga in my ears like earrings, Naga round my head as a garland, Naga round my body as a belt." There is something about Naga having three eyes, too.'

'Will you ask him if I can come with him when he gives them his milk?'

Dilip stopped and looked at Jake. 'Are you sure you really want to do that?'

'Quite sure,' replied Jake firmly.

'He says he will take you but I must not come.

My father would not allow it, he says, and I think he is right. Anyway, I admit I am afraid.'

'When does he go?'

'At sunset. That is in about two hours.'

Jake asked if there were any books on snakes in the house and Dilip showed him into his father's study where there were several reference books, encyclopedias and guides to India. Browsing through these, he found out a lot about cobras and other snakes. It was not encouraging to learn that about 40,000 Indians die each year from snake bite and the cobras account for more than any other snakes. However, he also read that they seldom attack unprovoked. Usually they are trodden on in the evening by people walking home from the fields or when they are disturbed without warning. No one seemed to know how long they could live, but there were endless legends about them and stories of cobras more than thirty years old. He learned that cobras can lay over fifty eggs which they guard in a nest made out of bamboo leaves and that the young are poisonous from the moment they hatch.

He was still busy reading when Dilip came to say that Ram Das was ready for him and anyway he had better get out of the study before Mr Barua arrived home.

Outside, the sudden tropical sunset was rapidly cooling the land and the light was fading fast. Ram Das was standing outside the kitchen door holding a wooden bowl of milk.

'He says you must be very quiet and do exactly what he does,' said Dilip. 'Please be careful. I have never done what you are going to do. No one here has. We are all afraid. Ram Das says he is only taking you because your grandfather was such a brave man and he believes you are brave, too.'

'Did he know my grandfather?' asked Jake.

'He was only a boy when he died, but yes, he has told me that he knew him. He remembers your grandmother, too.'

'Wow!' said Jake. 'I can't wait to tell her.'

Ram Das walked slowly ahead of Jake, carrying the bowl in both hands in front of him. He was making a ceremony of something he did by himself every day and yet he, too, felt that it was an important occasion. The other servants had always teased him for caring so much about the snakes, but they had none of them dared to come with him. Sometimes he worried about what would happen when he was gone. Unless the spirits of the snakes were worshipped properly they would leave. Then they would not be there to protect the house and it would be overrun by rats and mice and other, smaller snakes.

As they neared the great tree, Ram Das began to sing very softly. At the same time, he swayed slowly from side to side. Jake found himself doing the same. The tree was huge and its massive trunk was covered with creepers. Ferns and succulent parasitic plants grew out of every crevice, so the bark was only visible in a few places. From the first branches hung lianas, long rope-like plants which seemed to grow from both the top and the bottom, where they entered the earth. They almost formed a screen around the tree. It was darker behind them and, as Ram Das went past them to enter the round space between the lianas and the tree, Jake paused and peered in while waiting to let his eyes become accustomed to the gloom.

Still singing, but almost inaudibly now, so that his voice was now more like the buzzing of a swarm of bees, Ram Das lowered the bowl to the ground, bowed three times and stepped backwards to stand beside Jake. For a while nothing happened. Then Jake saw a slight movement among the creepers covering the trunk of the tree. They seemed to be rippling in two parallel lines. He watched, holding his breath, as the two ripples reached the ground together and the two largest snakes he had ever seen emerged from the vegetation and glided out towards the bowl. They were about two metres long, one slightly thicker and longer than the other. When they reached the bowl, they both dipped their heads into it and Jake distinctly heard the sound of their first sip.

He let his breath out with a rush, having forgotten he was holding it. Instantly, both snakes stopped drinking and reared up a third of their length above the ground. Their heads, which had been mere bulges at the front of their bodies, flattened out into wide hoods and they swayed fast from side to side. Jake could see the glint of their little eyes staring towards him and their forked tongues darting in and out. It was clear that they were trying to see who or what had disturbed them. He froze with terror and, had they moved towards him, he would have been unable to run away. Then Ram Das began to sing again, and he started to sway at the same rate as the snakes. Gradually the pace of the swaying slowed and their heads began to sag towards the ground. At the same time, their hoods vanished, their eyes stopped staring so hard and soon their tongues were reaching out towards the milk again. Ram Das touched Jake on the arm and they both walked very slowly backwards until they were well away from the tree.

At supper Jake asked Mr Barua to tell him about the big tree. Dilip's father was always pleased to be asked things and enjoyed showing how much he knew about all sorts of strange subjects.

'It's interesting that you should ask that,' he began. 'The tree is a sort of fig called a pipal but we also call it the bo tree. It is a sacred tree to Buddhists because it was under one of these trees that the Buddha sat and attained enlightenment. That one was in the state of Bihan and now there is a big temple and many pilgrims go there. It is one of the holiest of places. Our tree is not so holy, but the locals do practice some ceremonies here. Sometimes we catch local women walking round the tree in the night because they believe it will bring them boy children. Also we find they leave images and offerings there. It is better not to go near to the tree yourself as it is inhabited by cobras. I believe old Ram Das gives them milk but I do not encourage him. However, I cannot stop him either as he has lived here much longer than I have. Dilip is forbidden to approach the tree and it is the one rule he has always obeyed ever since he was little, as he knows the snakes could kill him if he disobeyed.' And Mr Barua looked fondly at his son.

That night, Jake went out and sat on the veranda after everyone had gone to bed. He could see the big tree from there and he gazed at it for a long time, wondering how he was ever going to get past the snakes and reach the treasure. After a while, the moon rose and flooded the garden with light. Although it was not yet full, it was so bright he could see everything almost as well as in the day. Even the colours of the flowers in the many flower beds showed up. Beyond them, below the little hill on which the bungalow stood, lay the neat rows of tea bushes with scattered trees among them to give shade from the sun. The moon itself had just appeared from behind the steep, forested hills which rose up from the edge of the plantation. With its appearance the night noises seemed to get much louder. There were crickets chirping constantly and a whole lot of other chirps and peeps which might have been birds or bats or frogs or more insects. The companionable noises reminded Jake of the nights he had spent on the Amazon the year before.

Looking back at the bo tree, he glimpsed something which made him stand up and hurry to the edge of the veranda. Staring into the night, he was sure he had seen something move away from the tree across the lawn. For a time he could see nothing, just the dappled shadows where the moonlight filtered through the leaves on to the lawn below. Then, quite clearly, he saw two very long dark objects slither side by side across an open patch. Without thinking, he walked out on to the grass and began to follow them.

It was surprisingly easy. The two huge snakes seemed to be travelling over a well worn and familiar route. Their speed was much slower than walking pace and he was able to stay well back while still keeping them in sight. They reached one of the paths made from beaten earth that bordered the lawn. Gliding smoothly over the brick edging, they turned together and continued down the hill towards the pond.

Suddenly, they both stopped and their heads turned as one to the left. A particularly loud croaking, unmistakably the sound of a large frog, was coming from a spot not far from the path. One of the snakes peeled off while the other continued. Not wanting to get between them, Jake waited. The croaking seemed to be getting louder and louder as he listened. Then, without any warning, it stopped dead. As though in sympathy, the whole garden went silent for a moment, too, before the night noises started up again.

Jake stayed still and after a while he saw the long thin shadow slide back on to the path again. Only now there was a distinct bulge behind the head. Just as he was about to move on, he saw another shape slip out of the shadows and follow the second cobra. For a moment he thought it must be another sort of snake, one that was much shorter but about the same thickness. Then, as it stopped and stood up for a moment on its hind legs, he saw that it was an animal about the size of a cat, only longer and thinner. Although he had never seen one, he guessed it must be a mongoose. He had read *The*

Jungle Book and remembered the story of Rikki-tikki-tavi. He knew that snakes and mongooses are natural enemies. Now he watched as it stalked the cobra until it was barely a metre behind it. The tip of the snake's tail was flicking from side to side as it moved along and this seemed to fascinate the mongoose, which reached out to pat it, like a kitten following a piece of string.

Suddenly the cobra became aware of its attacker. It wheeled around in one fluid movement and reared up to a third of its length to tower above the small animal. At the same time it expanded its hood and Jake thought how terrifying it must look if you were much smaller and below. But the mongoose just seemed excited and began to dance around like a boxer in the ring. It would pretend to dart at the snake as if to bite, then withdraw so fast that there was no time to strike. By comparison the cobra began to seem almost ponderous and moreover it still had a distinct lump below its head where the body of the frog was lodged in its throat. That must be slowing it up, Jake thought, and anyway, he had a feeling that a mongoose usually wins a battle with a snake. He would have thought that this snake would be more than a match for such a small adversary, being at least three times its size, but it began to look as though the snake was tiring and the little animal seemed to be working itself up for the kill.

Just then, another figure entered the scene. Somehow the cobra's mate must have heard or sensed the life and death battle going on behind it on the path. Moving fast over the ground, it came round behind the mongoose and so had its back to Jake. When it reared up he could see the extraordinary markings on the back of its hood. They were like eyes or spectacles in the back of its head; Jake stepped back as the eyes seemed to be looking at him. But all the attention of both snakes was concentrated on the mongoose and now it was being attacked from both sides. The tables had turned and the little animal was clearly on the defensive, leaping desperately from side to side to avoid the darting, and lethally poisonous fangs. With a squeak of annoyance it suddenly darted sideways and bounded off into some bushes.

The snakes moved slowly towards each other and then, in a gesture which Jake was convinced showed real tenderness, they both rose up again and coiled one around the other for a moment before dropping to the ground and slithering off down the path. Jake followed them at a distance until they reached the pond. There, without pausing, they both entered the water and began to swim out towards the little island with the duck house on it.

I'm never going to have a better chance than now thought Jake.

He turned and began to run back towards the tree.

10
The Tree

Jake was going to need a torch. Brave as he felt, there was no way he was climbing a tree in the dark, especially one which might have more snakes in it. He ran to the house and very quietly made his way to his room. Everyone seemed to be asleep, including Dilip, as he looked through the open door between their rooms. Rummaging in his bag without turning the light on, he found the little pencil torch his mother had given him. He remembered her saying, 'I'll bet this comes in useful. From what I've heard, the electricity in India is often off.' She would not be happy if she knew what he was about to do. He could also remember promising faithfully not to do anything dangerous and, for a moment, he felt guilty.

It was too late to stop and think now. He must hurry. The big snakes were happy catching frogs and perhaps a duck or an egg or two down at the pond, but there was no knowing how long they would stay there. He thought of waking Dilip to keep a look out for him but decided it would take too long. Instead, he took a deep breath and ran back out on to the veranda and across the lawn to the foot of the great bo tree. Pausing only for a second to gather his nerves, he pushed through the curtain of hanging lianas and entered the dark chamber behind.

Here he needed his torch. The thin beam showed him the creepers climbing up the trunk. Some of the them were as thick as his wrist and looked almost like snakes. He took hold of one gingerly and began to climb. It was not difficult; there were plenty of handholds and places for his feet. The hard part was keeping his mind off wondering each time he moved what he was about to touch. The creepers and the ferns brushed against his face and there was a strong, pungent smell. He wondered if it was the smell of tree or of snake. He held the torch in his mouth and a couple of time he stopped to shine it above him as he planned his route. Pushing through a particularly dense patch of under-growth with his eyes shut to avoid debris getting into them, he was surprised on opening them to find that it was light again. He had reached the fork, from which two massive branches grew while the main stem continued upwards. It was from these branches that most of the lianas hung and now he was above them. The branch he had reached was so big that he could stand up on it without needed a handhold. He did so and shone the torch around.

'In a hole in the first fork,' Granny Maisy had said. It must be somewhere pretty close to here, thought Jake.

Where his branch joined the main trunk there was a thick mass of vegetation which looked as though it might be concealing a hole. With the torch held in his mouth, pointing forward and lit, he parted the plants with his hands and looked in. It seemed to be a kind of nest made of bamboo leaves and twigs. When he pointed the torch down to the bottom he saw that he was right. There was a pile of whitish eggs. They seemed big and there were an awful lot of them. For a moment Jake wondered what sort of bird they could possibly belong to. Then, in the same instant, he heard the hissing and saw the hatchlings. They were not chicks at all; they were little cobras. There were about half a dozen that had hatched and they were unmistakable; perfect miniature replicas of the parents he had been following. Two or three had their tiny hoods raised and were ready to strike. Already at birth they were longer than Jake's hands. These he swiftly withdrew, dropping the sides of the nest back into place and stepping across it on to the other branch.

Now a real sense of urgency which was close to panic gripped him. He was sure the parents would not leave their offspring for long and they would not be pleased if they found him here on their return.

There was a hole where this branch met the trunk. Bending down, he shone the torch in. There, an arm's length inside, lay a tin box. For a moment Jake just stared at it. Then, taking a deep breath and praying nothing else lived in the hole, he reached in and put his hand on it. The tin box came away as though it had been placed there the day before. Without even looking at it, Jake put it inside his shirt, clamped the torch between his teeth again and hurled himself off the branch. He half fell, half scrambled down the trunk, scratching himself several times on the way but oblivious to everything now except his terror of meeting the cobras on their way back.

As soon as his feet hit solid ground he ran. Not pausing to find a gap in the lianas he plunged through and kept running across the open space towards the house. Only when he was safely back on the veranda did he stop and lie down, panting to get his breath back. A few seconds later, he was on his feet again tearing his shirt off, the tin box falling to the floor as he did so. There must have been more of the biting red ants somewhere up the tree because, once again, his body was covered in them. He spent some time finding and squashing all he could;

then, wearily, he picked up the box and tiptoed back to his bedroom.

Although he was exhausted and longed to lie down and go to sleep he dared not do so. He was covered in mud and leaves and he would make a mess which it would be hard to explain away. In the bathroom he dropped his clothes in a pile. At least they would be taken care of. He had become used to finding everything washed, pressed and returned almost before he took it off. Then he washed carefully under the shower which soothed his bites and removed the remaining ants. At last, putting the box under his pillow wrapped in a towel and deciding not to open it until the morning, he lay down and was instantly asleep.

11
Treasure

You are a lazy bones!' shouted Dilip, jumping on to Jake's bed and waking him up with a start. 'It is nearly lunchtime. I wanted to wake you but my parents said you must still be tired after your journey and I was to let you sleep. Now it is time to get up.'

'I *was* tired,' answered Jake, 'but not because of the journey. I was out most of the night and I got the treasure. Look!' and he held out the tin box.

'Golly!' exclaimed Dilip. 'How did you do it?' and Jake told him as he got dressed. By the time he had finished, Dilip was more impressed than ever and both boys were itching to open the box but had to wait until lunch was over. Throughout the meal they kept catching each other's eye and going silent with anticipation. Luckily, Mr Barua was full of a long story about a major problem he was having with the tea harvest. There was a new disease which he had never met before and he was having to spend all his time down at the factory testing samples. Both he and Mrs Barua were very worried and this meant that they had no time to be suspicious about what the boys were up to.

At last lunch was over. Back in Jake's room they fetched the box from where they had hidden it under his mattress, spread out the towel to catch the dirt which still clung to its sides and started looking to see how to open it. The box had once been black but was now a dull rusty red. It was fastened by a bar which slid between two channels, but everything was so rusted up that there was no way it could be removed. They tried scrubbing it with a nailbrush from the bathroom but as soon as they put any pressure on the lever it broke off. The only way to get in was to use the screwdriver attachment on Jake's Swiss Army knife to prise the box open. The hinge of the lid snapped off and the two boys looked in.

A folded piece of cloth filled the box. They lifted this out and unwrapped it. The material was some sort of oil cloth, which still felt sticky. Inside it was a bag made of soft leather with a drawstring, and a thick sealed envelope with nothing written on it. Jake pulled the string on the bag and tipped its contents on to his bed.

There was only one thing in the bag and the two boys stared at it for some time without saying anything. Then Dilip said, 'Jake, that is a proper treasure, I believe. Do you think it is real?'

Lying on the white sheet was a single red jewel which, even in the dim light of the bedroom, seemed to glow. It was about the size of Jake's thumb but round like an egg. Some of its surface was rough and opaque, but other parts were clear and it seemed that you could look deep into its centre. Each of the boys picked it up and felt the weight and the beauty of it.

'What is it, and why did your grandfather have it?' asked Dilip.

'Let's open the envelope,' said Jake. 'Perhaps that will tell us.'

The letter was written boldly in black ink. Some of the paper had gone brown, but it was still easy to read. This is what it said:

TO WHOM IT MAY CONCERN
Whoever opens this box must do exactly as I say.
If my wife Maisy opens it, she must put everything back, hide the box somewhere safe as I told her to, and go back to England. The safety of our child is more important than anything else.
If anyone else opens the box, I want them to return it to where it belongs. It comes from the village of Kubteh which lies right on the border of Burma. I have just come from there and the Japanese are only a day behind me. The stone is from the idol in the temple and it is sacred to the people of Kubteh. They asked me to look

after it for them as they knew the Japanese would steal it. I promised them that I would return it to them when the war was over.

If I die without doing so and you who find this box do not return it for me, the people of Kubteh will not forgive you.

Signed: George Beckett 14th March 1944.

Jake and Dilip stopped reading and Jake took the letter back. Very slowly, he folded it and put it back in the envelope.

'I suppose you are now going to try and do what your grandfather demands,' said Dilip quietly. 'I know you too well already to try and persuade you not to. We must just find a way.'

'Thank you, Dilip,' replied Jake. 'You are a good friend.'

'I'll tell you what,' Dilip was embarrassed. 'Why don't we go and let me introduce you to Rajah? That will give us time to work out a plan.'

Hiding the box under his mattress again with the jewel inside, Jake caught up Dilip who had already persuaded his mother to tell Singh to drive them to the farm in the foothills where his elephant was kept. Because they could not talk about what they wanted to talk about, they listened instead to Singh's cheerful chatter. He had completely recovered from his hurt feelings and carried on in his usual way, describing what they saw along the route.

'This river,' he said, as they crossed over a rickety plank bridge, 'I remember from when I was a boy. Then it was a raging torrent. Now you see. Almost no water. It is those bad men cutting down the trees in the hills. No one can stop them and the river dries up.' Soon after, they had to pull into the side to let past two huge lorries piled high with whole tree trunks. Singh waggled his head and shook his fist at them, but Jake noticed he waited until the lorries were well past before doing so.

They met elephants twice coming down the road towards them. The first had chains hanging from it which dragged along the road.

'That one has been stealing trees,' said Singh knowingly.

The next was carrying a massive load of grass fodder and looked like a moving haystack. They had to stop and pull right into the side to let it past. The boys laughed nervously as the enormous creature approached them. Even the head was partly covered, a kind of thatch hanging down over the great beast's eyes, so that it seemed to be feeling its way with its trunk. The elephant stopped as it drew level with the Land Rover and suddenly it became quite dark, since bushes blocked the light on one side and dry grasses on the other. Jake, who was sitting next to the window, put his hand up to wipe the

windscreen and froze as his hand touched something rough and crinkly.

'Dilip,' he whispered. 'I think I am touching
the elephant!'

'Be very careful,' urged his friend, also in a
whisper. 'Elephants can get very angry if they
are frightened.'

'I'm the one who's frightened,' said Jake.

'Please don't be.' There was a quiet authority
in Dilip's voice that Jake had not heard before.
'She will know what you are feeling. Just stroke
her trunk and give her a present if you have one.
Here, give her this apple. My mother gave it to
me as we left. Elephants like apples.'

Dilip, who was sitting in the back, passed the
apple to Jake, who had begun to stroke the
trunk. He could see the end now weaving about
like a snake, examining the dashboard and the
roof. When it turned towards him, he gently
placed the apple between the flared nostrils at
the end, which seemed to be sniffing him. By
inhaling, the elephant held the apple in place
and withdrew its trunk from the window to pop
the apple in its mouth. A couple of seconds later,
while contented crunching sounds came from
outside, the trunk was in again, clearly asking for
another. This time it went past Jake and began
to examine Singh, who Jake realized was sitting
rigid with fear and staring straight ahead. The
trunk seemed puzzled. There was no friendly

stroking hand and certainly no apple. Curling round in front of Singh's face, the end of the trunk seemed about to clamp itself on to his nose and Singh leaned back as far as he could, his eyes fixed on the snake-like object. Instead of touching his nose, there was a sudden blast of hot wet air from the end. Singh panicked and pressed both hands on the horn which sounded loud in the enclosed space. But that was nothing to the deafening sound of trumpets which came from the elephant as it withdrew its trunk and began to lumber off. The Land Rover rocked from side to side and for a moment it felt as though it was going to tip over. Then the light flooded in again and, turning round, the boys could see a speeding haystack trundling down the road, its anxious owner running along behind.

The boys were laughing hysterically, both with relief and because it was such a ridiculous sight, but Singh started the engine with shaking hands and drove on as fast as he could. Nobody said anything for a few moments. To break the silence, Jake asked Dilip, 'How did you know it was a she elephant?'

'In India only the males have tusks. It was lucky it was a she. Otherwise we could have been in trouble. You were very silly to blow the horn, Singh,' and for once Singh looked thoroughly ashamed of himself.

'I am sorry,' replied the contrite driver, 'but I have not been so close to an elephant before and I was very frightened.'

'Well you are going to meet my Rajah soon and if you show him you are frightened he will throw you into the river.'

The farm where Rajah was kept was a collection of huts in a patch of forest beside some waste land leading down to another dried-up river bed.

'There is Rajah!' shouted Dilip as they drove up. Jake saw a small elephant standing in a patch of shade, picking up leaves from a pile in front of him. He paid no attention to them as they climbed out of the Land Rover until Dilip appeared. Then he stopped eating, turned towards them and put his trunk straight up in the air.

'Look!' cried Dilip delightedly. 'He is saluting me. I taught him to do that.'

12
Rajah the Elephant

Rajah was less than half grown. 'He is the same age as me,' said Dilip. 'That is thirteen years old. He was given to me when I was three years old and he will probably live for as long as I do. He was born wild but his mother was killed when he was still a baby. We have grown up together.'

Dilip walked over to the elephant and gave him a hug. In return Rajah curled his trunk around the boy's back. They stood still for a moment and then Dilip stood back and gave a sharp command which sounded to Jake like 'Hit!' Immediately Rajah began to collapse. First, he sat down, almost like a dog after being told to sit; then extending his front legs, he seemed to slide forward until his chest was on the ground.

At once, Dilip climbed up on to his back and settled himself behind Rajah's big floppy ears. With his bare feet he kicked hard at the point where the ears joined the elephant's neck while at the same time shouting, 'Tah!'

With a good deal of heaving and grunting, Rajah got to his feet and was urged to start walking.

'Let's give him a bath,' said Dilip. 'Then we can both have a swim at the same time. Here, catch my shirt, please. I don't want to get it wet.'

Both boys were wearing shorts and so, when Rajah had made his way gingerly down the steep bank into the river and Jake had also removed his shirt, they were able to swim around the elephant, scrubbing the mud and dust off his back with bunches of leaves and pieces of a special creeper which lathered just like soap.

'He likes his bath,' said Dilip. 'I wish I could give him one every day but I am only able to visit him, once or twice a week and he gets lonely. I really ought to find a way of spending a whole week with him. He still has a lot to learn.'

This remark started Jake thinking and all the time they were playing in the water his mind was not entirely on the job. Rajah seemed to notice this and, after dipping his trunk in the water for a while, pointed it at Jake and suddenly showered him with a great deluge of water. This started the boys off splashing the elephant and for a while there was chaos as the three of them rolled and tumbled in the warm water of the river. Jake had to shake himself to realize he was actually playing safely and happily with an animal quite big enough to crush him with a single blow if it felt so inclined. But Rajah clearly liked and respected his master. Dilip only had to shout one of the words of command and, however excited and naughty the young elephant was being, he would immediately stop what he was doing and wait for further instructions. Later, as they lay on the bank and watched Rajah lying almost completely submerged in the river, Jake asked about the training.

'Did you have to punish Rajah often when you were training him?'

'No, I was lucky. Sometimes it takes a long time to make them do what you want. And you have to win, to show them that your willpower is greater than theirs. Otherwise it would always be very dangerous working with your elephant. If he was in a bad mood he would not do what you ask and if he was angry he might kill you. But Rajah has always been good. Also, I was lucky and I had Omar to help me train him. I wish you could have met him. He was your grandfather's elephant man and he could have told you lots of stories about him. But he died last year and now Rajah and I have to learn from each other.'

'I've been thinking,' said Jake. 'Why don't we go to Kubteh on Rajah?'

Dilip stared at him. 'Do you think you could ride him without falling off?' asked Dilip after a pause, and Jake, who had been holding his breath, waiting to see what his friend would say, breathed again with relief, knowing that his plan was going to work.

'Let's see,' he said and jumped into the river, landing with a splash on Rajah's back. The startled elephant, whose feet were resting on the river bed, leapt half out of the water, which streamed off his sides like a waterfall. Jake fell forward and reached out to clutch the ears and hang on for his life. Alarmed by Jake's unusual riding position, Rajah took off upstream, bounding in slow motion through the restraining water. All Jake could do was close his eyes and grip the leathery flaps of the ears with all his might as great bucketfuls of water crashed over him.

At last the elephant reached a deeper stretch of the river and stopped bounding as his feet could no longer reach the bottom. Jake thought his troubles were over, then realized with horror that Rajah was about to dive. Taking an even firmer hold on the ears, he just had time to draw in a gulp of breath before they submerged. Luckily the river was not very deep and soon he could feel that they had reached the bottom. Opening his eyes for a moment, he could just see that the animal he was clinging to was dancing along the riverbed in slow motion, a bit like pictures of an astronaut on the moon. Just as his lungs were beginning to burst and he thought he would have to let go and try to swim up to the air, the elephant seemed to push himself upwards and they both burst out of the water, surfacing like a submarine and both gasping for breath. Now swimming became hard work and so Rajah slowed up and eventually stopped, treading water in mid stream. Jake could now open his eyes fully and look up. Cautiously, he let go of the ears, sat up clear of the water and then stood up to wave at the small crowd which had gathered on the bank. He heard a distant cheer and decided it would make sense to leave the elephant and go ashore. Diving in, he started to swim.

It was further than he had thought and he realized that the current was carrying him downstream from the group of watchers. Jake wondered why they were still waving energetically. Suddenly, he felt what for a ghastly second he thought was a snake pass under his body; then, incredibly, he was out of the water and moving fast towards the shore, born up on Rajah's trunk. When they reached the bank, he was gently deposited on the ground. Dilip rushed up with an expression half of terror, half of laughter on his face.

'Are you all right? I have been so frightened for you. It looked so dangerous, but I knew Rajah would not hurt you.'

'Would you say I could ride an elephant now?'

asked Jake with a grin and Dilip fell on him with a shout of relief that all was well. They rolled together down the bank wrestling and ended up in the water yet again. Rajah watched them and Jake could have sworn there was a twinkle in his eye.

Much later, after drying their wet clothes in the sun and being given some tea by the couple who ran the farm and looked after Rajah, Dilip said to Singh, 'You had better wait here with the car. We are going to take Rajah for a walk.' Singh, who had kept well away during the fun and games in the river, was only too happy to oblige.

'We are going to have to make a careful plan,' said Dilip. 'My parents would never let me do what we want to do, but maybe we can pretend we are doing something else.'

'Exactly!' agreed Jake. 'Why don't we ask if we can go camping for a few days? After all, I am very keen to see as much of the natural history of this place as possible, aren't I?'

'If you say so,' answered Dilip with a grin, 'but I've got an even better idea. The forest behind here has just been made into a nature reserve and I know the new Chief Ranger. I'm sure I can persuade him to let us camp there – and then to be too busy to keep a very close eye on us. Now we had better go home and see whether my parents fall for it.'

They arrived back at the bungalow to find

long faces all around and Dilip's father in a very depressed and worried state. The news from the factory was even worse than he had feared and it looked as though he might lose a quarter of the crop. As a result Mr Barua hardly listened as the boys began to explain their plan.

'Yes, yes,' he said impatiently. 'Do whatever you like. I really have no time for such things at the moment.'

'But won't it be dangerous for them by themselves in the reserve?' asked Mrs Barua anxiously. Dilip said later it was the first time he had ever heard his father be rude to his mother.

'Don't be a silly, woman,' he snapped. 'Dilip is well able to look after himself and Jake is an experienced camper.'

As a result, it was all easier than they had dared hope and, anxious not to anger her husband again, Mrs Barua agreed without arguing to them helping themselves to anything they wanted from the kitchen.

By the time they went to bed, the boys had packed enough food for a week in one big canvas bag and some basic camping gear in another. As Dilip kissed his mother goodnight, he whispered in her ear, 'Why don't we get out of the way tomorrow morning? I'm sure Daddy will be happier if we are not here to bother him.'

'You are probably right,' sighed his mother.

'I'll tell Singh to be ready to drive you.' The boys tiptoed out of the room, expecting at any moment to be asked to spell out in more detail what they planned to do.

'We didn't even have to tell a little lie,' gasped Dilip. 'My father really must be very worried.'

13
The Forest

Back at the farm Dilip and Jake explained to the couple that they were taking Rajah away for a week. They said they would be in the nature reserve with the Chief Ranger so there was no need to worry about them. However, they left a sealed letter with them saying that in case they were delayed it was to be given to Dilip's parent. In this letter they revealed where they were really going so that if everything went terribly wrong people would at least know where to look for them.

'I do hope my father never reads this,' Dilip whispered to Jake. 'This is something I feel he might not forgive me for.'

They asked Singh to come back for them in exactly a week and declined his kind offer to come with them.

'You boys are not fit to be out in the this jungle by yourselves, you know,' he said. 'You need someone like me who is experienced in these matters.' But he did not argue and seemed quite

relieved when they insisted that they would be
fine.

'After all,' said Dilip, 'it is a nature reserve.'

'That is what is bothering me,' replied Singh.
'Nature reserves are where animals live and you
cannot trust animals.'

On the whole, the boys decided, they would
be much safer without him, although they did
have a momentary pang of doubt as they
watched him drive away.

The two canvas bags were joined by a strong
leather strap and Rajah did not mind their
weight at all when they were slung across his
back. When the boys both climbed on, however,
he did put his trunk back and feel them with it
before heaving himself to his feet. Then, with a
cheery wave to the couple and a quick glance at
the large-scale map he had pinched from his
father's office, Dilip gave a couple of kicks
behind Rajah's ears and the elephant moved off
at a stately pace.

Jake was not very comfortable perched
behind Dilip. There was nothing to hold on to
except his friend, who seemed to have better
balance, so that Jake felt foolish clinging to him.
After a while he slipped off and walked along
beside instead. This was fine while they were on
a wide timber track, but when they turned off
on to a narrow forest trail he had to walk
behind.

They had decided that they would visit an outpost at the edge of the reserve which lay on their route. From there they would send a message to the Chief Ranger saying they were going to camp nearby and he was not to worry about them. With any luck everyone would think someone else was looking after them and so they would be able to get on with their plan. This was to travel as fast as possible across country towards Kubteh, keeping well away from the few roads in the area. Luckily, the map showed a river running most of the way to a point quite close to the village and there seemed to be a faint track alongside it. In a straight line the whole distance was only about 40 kilometres and they reckoned they should be able to do that in two days, which would give them time to get back before their absence was noticed.

Their plan worked perfectly. There was only one sleepy guard at the outpost. He seemed quite pleased when they told him they would not be staying with him and making him look after them. He promised to give the Chief Ranger their message but they felt he was quite likely to forget. He directed them to the river they hoped to follow, which lay at the extreme eastern edge of the reserve. They told the guard that they would be camping somewhere around there for a few days and hurried on before he asked any questions.

Now Jake and Dilip were on their own, they were quiet for a while, each lost in his own thoughts as he considered the enormity of what they were doing. Soon they would be out of the reserve in completely strange country.

'We had better avoid meeting anyone,' said Dilip after some time. 'There are some dangerous people around this place. Also, I think it is illegal to go up to the Burmese border without a special permit.'

'Don't worry,' replied Jake with more confidence than he felt. 'I am sure it's all going to turn out all right.'

Soon after, they reached the river which was unmistakably the one on the map. It meandered along a wooded valley from which rose steep forested hills. Jake used his compass and to their relief found that it came directly from the east, which was the direction they were headed. They felt even better when they found that there was a track running along beside it. It was overgrown and sometimes Dilip had to dismount and lead Rajah round a fallen tree, but there was no doubt it was a track.

The river itself was clear and fast flowing, rushing over waterfalls into deep pools. It was tempting to stop for a swim but they pressed on, wanting to cover a much distance as possible before nightfall. It was Rajah who insisted on the first stop, determinedly walking down on to a gravel beach, putting his trunk into the water and using it to suck up water which he then drank noisily. Dilip dismounted by sliding down, holding on to the baggage straps, and he and Jake also had a good drink from the river and splashed their sweaty faces. It had been hot and sultry walking under the trees. Rajah wanted to have a bath but Dilip gave a sharp command before he could walk into the water and soak their bags. Instead they unpacked some rice wrapped in leaves, which they ate with delicious hot spices from small wooden containers with airtight lids. They lay on their backs to rest for a while and Rajah munched some tasty leaves. Then it was time to be on their way again and they trudged on, taking it in turns to ride on Rajah.

There was not much Jake had to do as, thanks to the path, there was nowhere for Rajah to go except straight ahead. But he began to get the hang of directing the elephant by kicking behind the ears with his bare feet. When he was riding, Dilip walked in front leading the way. Often Rajah would rest his trunk gently on Dilip's shoulder. Jake could see that there was real trust and affection between the boy and the animal.

They passed no one on the path, which seemed to be little used. There were occasional piles of elephant droppings, which Raja' sniffed with interest. Whether they were from wild elephants or loggers' beasts only he could tell. Once they passed a group of thatched huts, but they were dilapidated and abandoned and otherwise they saw no signs of human life. As the sun began to dip towards the horizon, they decided to stop and camp.

The river was still quite wide and they would have had to swim to cross to the other side. But there was a good place where they were able to get away from the track, so as to be out of sight if anyone should come along it. There were big grey rocks, against which Rajah became almost invisible, and they found a perfect spot between them where there was a natural platform on which they decided they would sleep. Upstream of the big rocks was a large area of tall grass and reeds. It was low ground, a flood plain where the river had changed its course, making a sharp bend so that the area was bounded on three sides by water.

They unloaded the bags and Rajah plunged happily into the river, splashing, snorting and showering water all over the place. The boys, who were feeling quite tired, gathered some wood, lit a fire – they had remembered to bring matches and so Jake did not need to demonstrate his trick of using the magnifying glass on his Swiss Army knife to make fire – and began to cook some more of the rice, meat and vegetables they had brought. They spread some dry grass on the ledge and then put their blankets on top. With the bags as pillows, their beds looked inviting and they felt quite pleased with themselves.

Before eating, they had a wonderful swim with Rajah in the pool below the rocks, cooling off before washing off the dirt of the day with some soap Dilip's mother had made him promise to use. They spread their wet clothes out on the warm rocks to dry and then tucked in hungrily to the hot meal they had prepared. There was plenty of fruit in the bag so that by the time they had finished they were quite full. They even found some sticky cakes which they thought they had better finish before they disintegrated completely from being bounced about on the elephant's back.

'We must let Rajah have a good meal, too,' announced Dilip. Calling his elephant to him, Dilip dug out a length of chain from the bottom of the food bag. 'This is a hobble,' he explained. 'If I don't put it on he may wander away in the night. He doesn't like it very much so you must talk to him while I put it on.'

Jake took hold of the end of Rajah's trunk, which was extended inquiringly towards him, and blew very gently into it. He could see the elephant's eyes looking straight at him from about a metre away. It was a strange sensation, but Rajah seemed to like what he was doing and his ears had stopped flapping. Meanwhile, Dilip fastened the hobble, which had two simple snap catches, on each of the front legs, so that they were joined close together. 'Well done, you can stop now. What were you doing? I've never known him stand so still.'

'It's something I was taught by a farmer I know at home,' explained Jake. 'He told me that if you blow gently down an animal's nose it will know you and be your friend. It seems to have worked with Rajah.'

'Just a long as you don't forget that he is my elephant and try to steal him,' said Dilip.

'I'm hardly likely to want to take him back to England now, am I?' said Jake with a laugh, and they both watched as Rajah hopped off into the grass.

'He won't go far now,' said Dilip. 'He'll be far too busy eating and filling that fat tummy of his. Let's explore a bit before it gets dark. We call this elephant grass. It is easy to get lost in it, so we must be careful to follow a track and return the same way.'

It was exciting and rather frightening walking in the tall grass; it was at least twice their height, so that it was more like travelling through a forest than a field. Most of the time it was far too thick to push through away from the track, but after a while they came to an open area where there were patches of bare earth. On the far side of this clearing was a huge pile of grass and leaves, almost like a low house. It clearly was not a house, yet something must have made it. Jake looked inquiringly at Dilip, who shrugged his shoulders. Keeping very quiet and miming what he was going to do, Jake picked up a short length of wood lying on the ground and lobbed it right on to the top of the heap.

Immediately, there was a loud grunt from inside. The boys ran for the nearest thick bush and hid behind it. Nothing happened. Although Dilip looked nervous and tried to stop him, Jake threw another, bigger piece. This time there was an explosion of sound: snorts, grunts, squeals, all still without any sign of movement. Then a huge black pig burst out of the heap, knocking half of it down in the rush. Behind came four little black piglets and they all dashed off squealing into the long grass and disappeared. Jake and Dilip looked at each other and giggled nervously.

'Lucky they ran away from us,' said Dilip. 'Those pigs can be dangerous.'

Remembering a horrible experience he had in the Amazon jungle, Jake agreed heartily. Keeping much quieter than they had on the way there, they retraced their steps to the camp, catching sight of Rajah munching away happily as they passed.

It was nearly dark by the time they had put on sweaters, blown up the fire, piled on lots of wood and wrapped themselves in their blankets.

'This is fun,' said Dilip, 'but I do think we should be careful. I am a bit frightened, I admit.'

'Don't worry,' replied Jake, as he snuggled down into the grass bedding. 'I am too. But there's really not much to worry about. As you saw with those pigs, most animals want to get away from us even more than we want to avoid them. Anyway, it's always better in daylight.' And, very tried after a long and exhausting day, they both dropped off to sleep almost immediately.

14
Wild Animals

Something woke Jake before dawn. He could not remember what it was when he opened his eyes. Had it been something in a dream, or something real? He couldn't tell. But there was a grey light and a stillness which seemed unnatural, so he kept his eyes open and listened intently. There was something, a faint sound above the soft stirring of the stream and he knew he had to find out what it was.

Very gently, he pressed Dilip's arm and when he saw his eyes open he put his finger to the other boy's lips. Dilip's eyes opened very wide now and, at the same slow pace as Jake, he began to sit up. Together, they put their blankets to one side, stood up and step by gradual step started to climb the slope of the biggest rock beside them. When they were almost on the flat top, they crawled on their stomachs for the last few metres and then very slowly raised their heads to look out over the river.

At first, Jake could see nothing but the grey

mist rising from the water and the faint outline of the far bank. Then, so suddenly that he froze with shock and felt the hairs on the back of his neck tingle, he saw what had made the noise. A fully grown tiger, like a tabby cat seen through a telescope, was lapping up water just below them. It was crouched down on the stretch of beach, which was hardly bigger than the tiger itself, and it was on the same side of the river as they were. Only the rock they were lying on stood between them.

Without moving his head, Jake squinted sideways to find out if Dilip had seen it. The fixed expression and the staring eyes told him more than words could have what was going through Dilip's mind. There was nothing to do but lie very still and watch a sight seen by very few.

The lapping went on for some time, occasionally interrupted by pauses when a deep growling, which Jake supposed must be serious purring, could be heard. As last the big cat stood up and stretched sensuously, seeming to extend each limb until every tendon had been tested. Beside the place where it had been drinking was a rock pool which the tiger now inspected. There seemed to be something in it which the tiger wanted: a fish, or perhaps a frog, Jake supposed. Just like a domestic cat trying to scoop a goldfish out of a small bowl, the tiger dipped a paw into the water, scooped furiously and then, having failed to fish anything out, spent a lot of time shaking the paw dry, licking it and ignoring the pool. Suddenly its ears went up and it became absolutely motionless, its eyes fixed on the bushes lining the bank. Without appearing to move, it was there one moment and gone the next. The beach was empty and it might all have been a dream, were it not for the mass of deep pawmarks in all the soft spots.

'Phew!' said Dilip. 'That is one animal I would not like to meet face to face.'

'Nor would I,' agreed Jake. 'Why don't we catch Rajah and get well away from here. We might as well travel while it's cool. Then we might be able to have a rest when it's too hot.'

Rajah proved easier to catch than expected. In fact he practically hurried over to them when they called, almost as though he had been feeling lonely and was pleased to see them. It took no time to load up and soon they were on their way. From the start the elephant seemed nervous, jumping at sudden noises from the bush and looking around anxiously.

'I've never known him like this before,' said Dilip. 'It must be that tiger. Let's hope it doesn't decide to attack. They aren't supposed to unless they're injured or ill and that one looked in the pink of condition. Keep close anyway, just in case.' Jake, who was walking behind, found himself reaching up and holding on to Rajah's tail. The elephant didn't seem to mind.

Halfway through the morning they reached another large patch of elephant grass. They were just about to plunge into it when Rajah stopped dead and extended his trunk right out in front of him, smelling hard at something. Just then they heard the unmistakable trumpet of an elephant and they caught a glimpse of several dark objects beyond the grass.

'That looks like a herd of wild elephants,' said Dilip. 'I think we would be wise to keep away from those. They might not take kindly to a young stranger in their midst.'

They made a detour, so that they would be following the now steep river bank rather than cutting straight across the little plain. When they were about halfway round, the trumpeting from the wild elephants suddenly increased tenfold and seemed to be coming closer. There was a big cotton-tree on the edge of a small cliff above the river and they decided to shelter there from the sun and wait a while to see what happened.

The trumpeting and squeals became louder and they could feel the ground shaking as what was now clearly a stampede of elephants approached.

'Something must have frightened them badly,' whispered Dilip, as he manoeuvred Rajah behind the tree. 'Perhaps the tiger tried to get one of their babies.'

At that moment the first of the elephants came into view. She was a magnificent specimen, unmistakably the boss of the herd. Her trunk was held up in front of her and she was making a tremendous noise, as though leading a charge into battle. Behind her, clearing a wide path through the tall grass, came the rest of the herd. They were three and four abreast, almost like drilled troops, and Jake was astonished to see that each had its trunk on the back of the one in front. That must be so that they don't lose each other, he thought. The scene reminded him for a moment of a picture in *Babar and the Elephants*, a book he had loved as a child.

There were about forty animals in the herd, the final group being a less organized mob of young and babies, their mothers frantically urging them along. Then, at the very back, came two stately matrons. They were calm and gave an impression of great strength. No tiger was going to tackle those two.

When the leaders reached the river bank, they paused for a moment and then broke ranks, milling about to find the best way down. It was three or four metres down to the river and a sheer drop for as far as could be seen in both directions. The female boss chose a spot and began to break away the top of the bank with her forefeet. When she had made a wide dent in it, she sat down on her bottom and tobogganed to the river, entering the water with an impressive splash. The rest followed her without hesitation. If there had not been such a sense of panic and urgency, it would almost have seemed that they were enjoying themselves. They looked to Jake like children at an aqua park careering down a flume, screaming with excitement.

When they arrived on the scene, the young elephants were less brave about plunging down the slope and some needed an encouraging push from one of the adults. There was one very small baby which looked really lost and frightened. It was running around with its trunk held up high, looking for its mother and getting knocked over in the rush. The two old elephants moved into the mob to protect it, taking up position on either side. One touched it gently with her trunk while the other fended off an overexcited adolescent who was about the crash into it. At that moment its mother, who had been separated in the stampede and was clearly frantic with worry, rushed over, wrapped her trunk around her baby and pulled it to her. Immediately it started to nuzzle underneath her chest and, for the briefest of moments, it actually appeared to be having a drink of milk.

Then it was time to cross the river. All the others had slid down the bank and were swimming to the far side. Some had already reached it and were standing there, trumpeting anxiously to the rest. Only the three adults and the baby remained. The baby did not like the look of the slope. When pushed that way it squealed hysterically and tried to run back into the tall grass. Patiently, but with worried glances towards the grass, for this was, after all the most likely member of the herd to fall prey to the tiger, the three females tried again to drive the baby to the bank. But it was no good and Jake could see that they were all longing to join the rest across the river. I do hope they don't abandon it, he thought.

Just then the mother did an extraordinary thing. Scooping the baby up in her trunk, she lifted it off the ground, ran to the bank and slid down, holding it up in front of her. When they hit the water, she continued to hold her baby up as she dog-paddled furiously across to the other side. Jake and Dilip felt like cheering as she deposited it on the far bank and the rest of the herd crowded round to nuzzle it. But they stayed quiet and watched as the elephants formed up again and disappeared into the forest. They had all been so preoccupied with their own troubles that none of them had noticed Rajah and the boys, although they had passed within a few metres of them. Gradually, the muddy, churned-up stream of the river returned to normal, peace descended on the river bank and all of nature seemed to heave a sigh of relief that the drama was over.

The boys waited for some time to see if the tiger would appear. When it seemed safe to go on, they both climbed on to Rajah's back and he walked fast and quietly along the bank until they reached the shade of the forest again.

Towards evening they became convinced that they must be nearing Kubteh. The river was by now only a small stream and the ridge of hills which Dilip was sure marked the Burmese border, lay just ahead. The track had remained clear all the way and yet they had not met a single soul. The only signs of human life had been smoke rising sometimes from clearings up in the hills on either side.

They camped early at another good place, although there was less grass for Rajah to eat. While Dilip stayed to keep an eye on the elephant, Jake decided to go for a walk and explore the way ahead. He left the track and the stream, striking off towards the ridge. The forest was open and he could make his way easily through the clumps of undergrowth. He climbed a couple of low hills, made his way around a swampy area and came into some different country. The undergrowth was much thicker here. There were fewer big trees and he kept having to make detours. When he decided to go back to the camp, he realized his sense of direction had deserted him and he had no idea which way to go. He was completely lost. Everything looked the same and the sun was no help as, although it was still daylight, the evening was cloudy and he could not tell where the sun was.

Determined not to panic, he sat down and took out his compass. Of course he should have been looking at it ever since he left Dilip, but he had forgotten to do so and now he regretted it. Assuming the stream still ran from east to west, the ridge from north to south and he had gone to the left away from the track, then to get back he ought to head south west. But the terrain was so broken that he could not be at all sure this made sense. As he sat and tried to work out which way to go, he heard a cock crow. That, he thought, means people. Perhaps he was close to Kubteh after all.

So, instead of trying to find his way back, he followed the sound of the crowing. Soon it was quite close and, thinking there might be people about, he crept forward very cautiously. Peering round a tree he saw a beautiful bantam cock standing in a small clearing. Its colours were the brightest he had ever seen. There were bantams on the farm at home in England but none of them was a patch on this one. It had a bright red comb above an orange ruff, red wings and a green tail. Standing on tiptoe and arching its neck, it gave another splendid cock-a-doodle-doo. It was such a familiar and domestic sound that Jake stepped out into the clearing, expecting the cock to come over to him for food. Instead it gave him a horrified look and took off like a pheasant. It soared straight up into the air and flew off over the trees. Jake stared after it, puzzled. Chickens weren't meant to behave like that. Then it dawned on him. This had been no domestic bird but one of the ancestors of all poultry. It must have been a jungle fowl, the original wild chicken that he had crept up on. And that meant that he was no closer to people than before.

Jake decided to walk due south by his compass and he set off determinedly, trying not to panic. After a while he stepped out of the forest into a cleared field. This was certainly not somewhere he had been before, but it did mean there would be people about. Whether they would be friendly or not was, of course, another matter. He walked across the open space and found a well-used track leading away from it. This he followed, trotting now as the light was fading. Coming around a corner, he almost bumped into a big bundle of logs apparently bouncing along the path on its own. It was only when he stopped and looked more closely that he saw the girl bent double under an enormous load of firewood. She was too busy to notice him and he was able to follow her, keeping well behind.

Quite soon their path met a much wider one and then he was looking down on the thatched roofs of a large and well ordered village. It had to be Kubteh. There was nowhere else marked on the map for miles around.

15
The Village

What should he do now? Of course, the best idea would be to go back and fetch Dilip, who would be able to explain why they had come. The jewel was safe in one of the bags; they could produce it and give it back to the village. The trouble was, Jake had absolutely no idea how to find the camp and it was about to get dark. Even if he did go in the right direction, he was not likely to get back in time. He had not brought a torch, food or anything, except his knife. He began to feel very stupid, especially as Dilip would by now be very worried.

But he did not feel like just walking into the village and trying to explain in sign language where he came from and what he was doing there. That could be tricky. Singh's stories about headhunters came back to him and he felt a chill of fear. There was a big tree beside him and it looked easy to climb. Wanting a better view of the village he pulled himself up a hanging liana until he could stand on a massive branch. From there the village lay spread out below him. There were about twenty houses, all very big and thatched right down to the ground. In the centre was a low hill on which stood the biggest house of all. Next to it was another built in a different style. The sides were open and it looked more like a large bandstand. He could see people walking about, some water buffaloes grazing on the edge of the earth streets and some women drawing water from a well. They did this by pulling down one end of a long pole fastened to what looked like a tree trunk next to the well. The other end would then rise up, lifting a full bucket of water from the depths. From this they filled their earthenware pitchers. Jake had not had a drink for some time and the sight of the water slopping back into the well made him thirsty.

Just then he heard voices approaching. He lay down on the branch and tried to make himself invisible. A group of men came down the path. They were brown and muscular. Each carried a spear and had a long sharp knife like a sword hanging at his side. Jake had seen these back at the tea plantation and knew they were called *daos*. The men wore nothing but red loincloths and red bandannas tied around their heads. Each had a short, black beard and, as they drew nearer, Jake could see that their bodies were covered with tattoos. They looked extraordinarily fierce. Jake lay very still.

They stopped under the tree and talked animatedly. There seemed to be an argument going on, though Jake could not understand a word they said. One, a bigger scowling man, brandished his *dao* and Jake thought there was going to be a fight. But the others seemed to calm him down and he strode off muttering. The others talked for a bit longer, then followed him down the hill.

Jake lay in his tree for a long time, watching the village prepare for the night as darkness fell. He was hungry as well as thirsty now and he kicked himself for not having eaten something before setting out for his walk. It had not occurred to him that he would not be back within an hour. Now it was nearly midnight and he was beginning to feel desperate.

The village seemed to have gone to sleep. There were still one or two small oil lamps burning but he thought they were probably left to burn all night. He ached for a drink and decided he would have to find one whatever the risk. One way would be to make his way through the forest downhill until he found a stream. The moon had risen and it was quite light in the open, but under the trees it was still dark. He simply was not brave enough to grope his way through the forest in the dark. It was just too dangerous. The other alternative was to go to the well. He could see it clearly in the moonlight.

Gathering his courage, he slipped down from the tree, stretched his cramped limbs and set off towards the village. The path was wide enough to let the moonlight in and he had no trouble reaching the first house. It loomed over him like a giant haystack, casting a shadow through which he crept silently. His main fear was dogs, but he had seen none and heard no barking and so hoped he would not meet one.

The well was in the centre of the village. He had plotted his route carefully and he was soon beside it. The pole had a rope hanging from it. Heaving on this, he heard the bucket splash deep in the well as the far end began to rise. It was harder work than he had expected but, at last the bucket rose above the lip of the well. Now his problem was to get to it. If he let go of the rope the bucket would crash back down to water level again, probably making enough noise to wake the whole village. Some water slopped out of it tantalisingly as he considered what to do. The nearest building was the open-sided one which looked like a bandstand. Still pulling on the rope, he walked across and, to his relief, found that it just reached it. He tied the end securely to the bottom of a notched pole, which made a crude but effective ladder up to the building. Then he hurried over to the bucket. The water was cool and delicious. He drank lots and then poured the rest over his head, after which he felt much better. Looking down into the well, he could see the water glinting in the moonlight far below.

He walked back to untie the rope and, before doing so, glanced into the building to which he had attached it. What he saw made him freeze with horror for what seemed like several minutes. Just above his head was a long row of skulls, their empty eye sockets appearing to stare straight at him. Jake had never seen a real skull before but he had no doubt that these were the victims of headhunting raids. The *daos* that the men under the tree had been carrying would be able to remove a head with a single stroke. He was mad to have come into the village and he must leave at once, however frightening the jungle outside might be.

Just as he was about to move, he heard the sound of footsteps approaching. There was no time to lower the bucket or run away. There was nowhere to hide on the ground as the house stood on stilts and the earth was bare underneath. The only place to go, and he would have to be quick as he could see the stranger's legs on the other side, was up the notched pole and inside. He was up without a sound, then he stepped into the shadows and crouched down.

As the man came round the corner, Jake could see that it was the big bad-tempered man he had seen arguing with the others under the tree. He heard him give a grunt of surprise as he tripped over the rope and heard him muttering crossly as he untied it and let it go. As Jake had expected, the bucket dropped to the water with a loud crash, but no one seemed to take any notice, although a dog did start barking on the far side of the village. The man lurched off across the open space and Jake realized he was drunk. Lucky for me, he thought. If he was sober, he might have wondered why the bucket was left tied up.

Jake stood up and nerved himself to take a closer look at the skulls. They were not so frightening once he examined them. Certainly, none of them looked at all fresh; in fact they were dusty and crumbling with age. I'm sure they've given up headhunting now, he said to himself, but he was not able to convince himself completely, and the memory of those very tough-looking characters made him wonder. Walking very quietly down the row to count the skulls, he found there were 65. Above them, attached to the rafters, were the huge horns, and sometimes also the skulls of buffaloes. Scattered among them were the antlers of deer. The whole place began to look like some medieval baronial hall and Jake had an urge to giggle. But there were dark shadows up the farther end, where someone might be sleeping, and so he tiptoed that way very softly.

The sides of this end of the building were thatched and it was darker here. Two huge objects began to take shape as he drew near. One was long and low; the other towered up to the rafters and looked like a giant person. The first was a vast hollow tree trunk which lay on solid trestles. Jake wondered what it could be for. It was too irregular to be a canoe and the wrong shape to be a container for anything. Anyway, when he peered in he could see that it was empty.

The other object was more frightening even that the skulls, once his eyes became accustomed to the dark and he could see what it was: a colossal carved figure of a god with big, painted eyes and a very fierce expression that really made him feel that it was looking at him. It made him feel very small and insignificant, but as he gazed up at the face he noticed that there was an empty round hole in the middle of the giant figure's forehead.

'That,' Jake breathed aloud, 'is where the jewel came from!'

Although he had spoken very quietly, it had been enough to disturb someone who was sleeping in the building. Jake heard a rustle, as though a body had sat up; then the rustling of a blanket being thrown back and muttered voices as the waker woke another. It was time to hide, but where? The only place within reach was inside the big horizontal tree. Silently, Jake slid over the side and crawled down into the dark.

Outside he could hear voices and he didn't have to understand the language to know what they were saying. They were both men and one was clearly trying to convince the other that he really had heard something. The second voice was grumpy and sounded doubtful. As Jake lay absolutely still, they shuffled about the building for a time and then went back to bed. Silence reigned once more. Jake decided he was as well off where he was as anywhere. He would wait until it became lighter, then slip away from the village and find his way back to Dilip's camp.

For a time he slept. Then he woke suddenly and it was as though a bad dream was recurring, only he was not asleep. There was no chance that the animal crawling over his head was being dangled by a naughty Indian boy. There really was a large spider in the tree with him. He lay still, but it was hard to do and when he felt a sharp pain in his left ear, he jerked upright, banging his head violently on the 'roof' of the hollow tree.

To his astonishment, this set off an extremely loud booming sound, which went on for a long time, echoing around not only the building but also the whole village. It was such a surprise that he forgot the spider for a moment and clapped his hands to his ears to stop himself being deafened. Then he remembered that he was not alone and, as the sound began to die down he scrambled out over the side. Immediately, he was seized by the two men who had looked for him earlier and thrown to the ground. Help, he thought, now I'm for it.

16
The Ceremony

The men were shouting and soon the whole village seemed to have gathered around the house. Jake was manhandled roughly to the top of the steps and shown to the crowd. A growl of fury came from them when they saw he was a stranger. He was quite brown by now and his face had been coated with dirt and dust inside the tree trunk so he supposed he must have looked Indian. He was much too frightened to speak when they shouted at him and so, after a while, he was dragged down the steps and across to one of the large houses.

Thrust inside, he was surprised to find how spacious it was. There were several stone hearths placed at intervals along its length. These were being blown into life and this made enough light for him to see everything clearly. Above the fire, where the smoke made its way out through the roof, hung smoked meats and vegetables and other things in pots. Around the walls hung spears and bows as well as baskets and hats made of straw. The floor was of split bamboo, swept clean, and it felt warm and cosy. The atmosphere with which he was greeted was, however, anything but warm. Everyone was shouting at him and he felt it would not be long before someone hit him. They were extraordinarily angry and he began to be afraid that he had done something terrible, something worse than just being caught trespassing and possibly stealing.

Some of the children now began to take an interest in him. One small boy, braver than the rest, ran up and threw something at him. He thought the rest were about the follow suit but a beautiful young woman stepped in between him and the children and spoke to them rapidly and angrily. Then she turned on the men gathered around the entrance and, in gentler tones, seemed to be pleading with them. After some discussion, she seemed to get her way.

Everyone watched as she went up to Jake and, taking a woven rope down from the wall, tied it firmly but gently around his wrists. She then led him to a walled-off cubical at the side of the house, pushed him firmly inside and tied the rope to a strong upright supporting the roof. She picked up a piece of cloth and, spitting on it, wiped some of the mud off his face. This was something his mother had done when he was small and he had always hated it. He pulled away angrily and she smiled, looking at him curiously in the lamplight. Then, because he felt he had been rude, Jake smiled and tried to look sorry. The woman laughed outright at this, threw a woven mat and a blanket on the floor by the pole and indicated that he should rest. Without a word, she turned and walked out, pulling a bamboo screen shut and leaving him alone.

Jake tested the rope around his wrists, but she had tied it too well and he could not begin to undo it. He knew he should be trying to escape, but he was just too tired and so he lay down and went straight to sleep.

The woman woke him with a delicious bowl of hot rice and some small pieces of meat. She untied his hands and he wolfed it all down as she watched him. He was ravenous, having barely eaten on the previous day. She looked on with an amused smile, but this changed to anxiety when a man burst in and started shouting. She insisted that he was allowed to finish his meal, then he was again pushed roughly out of the house and into the open air. He had not realized how late it was and the bright sun made him blink.

The whole village was gathered by the well. They were sitting in neat rows, the men in front, women next and children at the back. Facing them, with their backs to the main street of the village and sitting on three stools were a very old man with a wispy grey beard in the middle and a pleasant-looking young man holding a strange carved stick next to him. On the other side, Jake was alarmed to see the big angry man who had seemed drunk the previous evening. The old man was dressed quite differently from all the other men of the tribe Jake had seen. For a start, he was wearing a bright red tunic which reached down to his knees. It was fastened with a broad belt made out of cowrie shells, the same but much larger than those he had collected at home at the seaside. On his head was a round hat made of tightly woven bamboo, so fine that at first glance Jake thought it was made of felt. At his side was a *dao*, much longer than the ones carried by the other men and sheathed in a beautifully carved wooden scabbard. On each of his forearms were long arm protectors, like little shields, woven in the same way as his hat. His face was covered in blue tattooing. This could be none other than the chief.

Jake was led up to stand in front of them. With his hands at his sides, he stood as straight as he could and tried to look them in the eye. He was sure that he was now on trial. Judging by their anger the previous night, his punishment was likely to be severe but he was determined not to show how frightened he was. The old man seemed to have a twinkle in his eye, though he looked stern enough. The angry man had his *dao* in one hand and looked ready to use it on Jake. The young man actually smiled at him but Jake didn't dare to smile back. The stick he was carrying had a bunch of curiously twisted strands of bamboo tied to the top. They were curled into all sorts of strange shapes and seemed to shake in the breeze, although the morning was still and windless.

The case began with the two young men who had caught Jake giving a vivid description of what had happened in the night. Although he could not understand a word that was being said, it was quite clear to Jake that they were making the most of it. They mimed how they had crept around the building and jumped on him. Jake longed to be able to say that they would never have found him if he hadn't given himself away.

Then they began to interrogate him. The old man asked him some questions in a gentle voice first and again he felt that if he could only explain himself he would be treated sympathetically. He kept trying to remember the few words of Hindi he had begun to learn at the tea plantation, but his mind was frozen with fear and he could think of nothing to say. Then the angry man leapt to his feet and began to shout into his face. Leaping about and waving his *dao* in the air, he screamed and yelled, working himself up into a real fury. Jake was beginning to think that his last moment really had come and that his head was going to be removed at a single stroke, to join the others in the building behind him, when he glanced over the old man's shoulder and his face broke into a broad grin. This confused the angry man who stopped jumping about and turned to see what had changed Jake's mood so suddenly. Then the whole village gave a gasp and rose to look and the old man and the young man also turned around in their chairs.

Coming up the middle of the village street was Rajah with Dilip riding proudly on his back. As they drew near, Jake could see that Dilip was trying to keep a straight face and look solemn, but he was not being very successful. He rode Rajah right next to Jake, shouted 'Hit!' and the elephant sank to the ground as gracefully as he was able. Dismounting, Dilip stepped up to Jake, put his hand on his shoulder and began to speak in a loud voice to the assembled villagers.

Jake watched their expressions turn from anger to amazement to joy, when he knew Dilip must be telling them about the jewel. When the time came, Jake went over to the bag hanging at Rajah's side and rummaged inside. Finding the pouch with the jewel in it, he carried it over to the old man and handed it to him.

The old man stood up so that the whole village could see. With trembling hands he pulled the drawstring on the pouch and tipped the stone out into his hand. When he held it up and it caught the sunlight, there was a moment of absolute stillness and then there came a roar of pure happiness. Suddenly, everyone was coming up to Jake and bowing in front of him, their hands held together in the Indian greeting 'namaste'. He smiled and thanked them in English, then went over to the woman who had looked after him and made the same gesture to her. This was greeted with another great cheer.

The young man with the staff came up to him and said in good English, 'Why did you not say you were English? I could have translated for you.'

'I didn't think there would be anyone here who spoke it,' Jake replied.

'Oh yes. There are several of us here who have been away to school and speak quite well. I have myself been to university. My name is Lanu. We are not as primitive as we look!'

'Do you still hunt for heads?' Jake asked.

'Oh no, absolutely not! We gave that up a long time ago. Mind you, if someone did something absolutely terrible, like disturbing our sacred skulls . . .' and he grinned at Jake, slapping him on the back.

'What is the thing I hid inside?' Jake asked.

'Ah, that was bad luck!' Lanu replied. 'You hid

in the *thom*. That is our drum with which we wake up the village if we are attacked or if there is a fire. You could not have found a better way of telling us you were here than by banging on that with your head! It is also the place where the bachelors in the village sleep, guarding the skulls, and so you stood no chance of escaping.'

The old chief now came up to Jake and Lanu translated for him.

'He asks me to thank you for returning the stone. He says you are now an honoured guest and he is sorry you were mistaken for a criminal.'

'Why does he wear a red coat?' Jake asked.

'That is because he is the chief. When the British first conquered this land about a hundred years ago, your soldiers wore red coats. They gave one to the man they recognized as chief and our Indian government has done the same ever since. Every three years our chief is entitled to a new coat.'

That evening there was an enormous feast. A water buffalo was slaughtered and cooked in great pots. The village was full of the smell of cooking and everyone was happy. At sunset everyone gathered around the skull house and watched as the old chief made a speech to the village god. Lanu again translated for Jake.

'He is explaining that the treasure was removed by your grandfather when he was a boy. He says he remembers him well: a great hero who fought against the Japanese and saved many people from being killed or imprisoned. He took the stone to save it from being taken by the Japanese, when we would never have seen it again. Now his grandson, who is just as great a hero, has come to return it. He says the village will always be your friends and will come to you anywhere in the world if you need them.'

The young man who had woken up when Jake was exploring the skull house then climbed up the side of the statue and placed the stone firmly back in its socket. It fitted exactly, leaving no doubt in anyone's mind that it was returning to its rightful home.

Throughout the evening Jake and Dilip went from house to house being offered food and treated as honoured guests. When they reached the hearth of the angry man, he dropped to his knees and bowed down. 'He is asking for forgiveness,' said Lanu. 'Are you going to give it to him?'

Jake, who felt he could get away with anything, took down a *dao* from the wall and held it over the man's head for some time while everyone watched in sudden stillness. Only when he saw the man's terrified face peer round and look up at him in anguish as he crouched did Jake relent. Tapping him gently on the shoulder, as though knighting him, he said, 'Tell him not to be so horrid in future,' and everyone laughed with relief when Lanu did so.

'You really are almost as naughty as me,' said Dilip that night after they had been given the best blankets and the most comfortable section of the bamboo floor in the kind lady's house. 'You are also very lucky that I found my way here so quickly.'

'I know,' said Jake with feeling.

17
The Return

That night Jake had a vivid dream. It was not like normal dreams as he could remember it clearly in the morning. But it was not like the one he had had when the old Indian jadugar had put him to sleep. This one just seemed to come to him. It was a happy jumble of people and faces. Granny Maisy was there, looking young and pretty as she must have been when she lived in India, and there was a tall man with a moustache who Jake knew must be his grandfather. They were holding hands and smiling at him. Other friends flashed past and they all looked pleased and happy for him. Only his father, who looked anxious and seemed to be listening for something, and his mother, who had her hands in the kitchen sink, then pushed back her hair with a soapy hand and looked as though she was crying, did not seem to be sharing his happiness. He awoke, knowing it was time to go home.

'We must go back now,' he said, and he gave Dilip a push as he woke him.

'I know. We will be lucky if my parents have not smelt a rat by now. The old man was saying that our journey was dangerous and we were fortunate not to meet any bad people on the way. He is going to send some of the young men of the village to accompany us.'

They had a tremendous send-off. Everyone came down the path as far as the river, cheering them, singing, banging on drums and making a terrific noise. The children who had been so ready to be beastly to Jake when he was a captive, now ran up to him with flowers and cakes. They made a great fuss of Rajah, who was well rested and had had a very good feed.

'Remember,' the old chief said and Lanu translated as they finally said goodbye, 'if you ever need any help anywhere in the world we will come to you. You have only to ask. We are in your debt for ever.'

Jake knew they meant it and he hugged the knowledge to himself as he and Dilip rode away together on Rajah with their escort of warriors running along in front and behind. One day he would see them again.

They moved fast through the day. Rajah, knowing he was heading for home, surged along at a sort of lope somewhere between walking and trotting so that those on foot had to run to keep up. At midday they rested for an hour, bathing in the river and sunning themselves on the rocks. Two of the warriors had been off hunting on the way and had reappeared with a young pig slung between them on a pole. This was singed over a fire to remove the hair, then roasted and cut up into small portions, which were wrapped in large leaves and packed away for eating in the evening.

They made fast progress. By late afternoon Jake, who had run most of the way while Dilip rode the elephant, was feeling pretty tired and he asked when they were going to camp.

'They say that we will reach the reserve tomorrow morning at this rate and so we can camp soon,' Dilip replied. 'We must wait here while some of the men go ahead a find a good site.'

After quite a long wait, during which the sun began to set and Jake wondered why they could not camp where they were as there was plenty of room by the river, the men came back. They had something important to tell and everyone crowded round them to listen. Jake waited impatiently.

'We have a problem,' said Dilip at last. 'There is a group of illegal loggers just ahead. They are very dangerous men and they have several elephants with them. Even if we tried to sneak past in the night, the elephants would hear us and raise the alarm. We cannot stay here because it is too close and they might find us. We cannot go

139

on and we do not want to go back. Some of the men want to attack. They are angry because they say this forest is theirs and these people are stealing the timber. Others say it is too dangerous because we have only spears and bows while they probably have guns.'

'What do you think we should do?' Jake asked.

'I don't know. Anyway, they would probably not listen to me. But, as the grandson of Mr Beckett, they would do whatever you ask.'

'Why don't we go and have a look?' Jake suggested.

As soon as Dilip translated this, two of the young warriors leapt up and offered to show them the way. Jake and Dilip followed them up a faint path leading away from the track and the river. After a short, steep climb they came to a ridge. There was a cliff on the far side from which they could look down into the loggers' camp.

Smoke was rising from a couple of fires and there seemed to be about eight men and boys squatting around them. Nearby were the same number of elephants. They were much bigger than Rajah, but they looked thin and unhealthy. They were all tied together in a line with heavy chains and they stood with their heads hanging down. Even from the distance of the ridge, Jake could see that they had bloody sores on their legs where the chains had rubbed them.

'What would those elephants do if they were free?' asked Jake.

'Perhaps they would return to the forest and join up with a wild herd,' answered Dilip. 'If elephants are well looked after they love their masters and would never run away. But these ones look so miserable . . .'

The friends looked at each other for a moment as the same thought took shape. 'Let's do it!' said Jake, and Dilip nodded.

'Life is going to be quite boring when you go back to England – I hope!' said Dilip. They grinned at each other, then crawled back and ran down to the others. Dilip made them all gather round and announced that Jake wanted to address them.

'My friends,' he said, feeling very self-conscious as Dilip translated, but at the same time knowing that the handsome, brave men sitting on the ground in front of him would do as he asked. 'I believe we have to fight these bad people. When the Japanese army came to try and steal your land from you, my grandfather helped you and in time they left. Now these men have come to steal your forests. I am not a man like my grandfather but I know he would want me to stand with you against your enemies.

'Let's creep into their camp tonight, free their elephants and drive the robbers away. They may have some guns, but you can steal those and throw them in the river. Meanwhile, Dilip and I will use Rajah to let us get close to the elephants. Once we have released their chains, we will stampede them through the camp. If we do this just before dawn, then we can be well away before they realize what has happened.'

This plan was discussed at length and everyone agreed it was a good one. They all spent a restless night getting prepared. Luckily they had food with them ready to eat without making a fire. There was lots of cold rice and the wild pig that had been killed on the way. They posted guards to watch the loggers' camp in case any should decide to walk up the path and discover them. This seemed unlikely as they could hear the noise of singing and shouting from where they were. It looked as though the loggers were getting drunk. This was good news.

The rest of the warriors sat and talked in quiet voices, sharpening their spears and sorting out their bows. Jake now had a chance for the first time to examine the bows more closely and he suddenly realized that they were quite different from any he had seen before. Also, he noticed that they seemed to have no arrows.

'How do these work?' he asked Dilip.

'They call them *gooti dhenu*, which means 'stone bow'. This tribe only uses this sort and they are very skilled with them. They fire small stones and pellets of hard earth instead of arrows. In this way they can knock down birds and small animals; they use their spears for larger ones, like the pig we have just eaten.'

Feeling a bit like some medieval monarch rallying his troops on the eve of a great battle, Jake walked among them in the moonlight to see if they were ready for the fight ahead. He could see that none of them was afraid and that they were eager for whatever the morning would bring.

'Will you ask them to try not to kill anyone, please,' he whispered to Dilip. 'Tell them that would only make trouble. But they can frighten them as much as they like so that they never come back.'

He watched the faces as Dilip translated and saw how some of the young men looked disappointed but the older ones nodded in agreement.

At three o'clock by Jake's watch they began to take up their positions. There was little to pack up, but they hid Rajah's saddle bags at a place they could find again easily beside the track. Then the young men who had been selected as the best and the quietest trackers began to crawl towards the camp. Jake and Dilip waited with Rajah until the first one returned carrying a rifle he had slid away from the side of a sleeping logger and they heard a faint splash as he threw it in the river.

Now it was time for them to do their stuff. Holding on to Rajah's trunk and whispering into his ear to be very quiet, they crept very slowly towards the line of elephants. It was a tremendous risk to take Rajah, they knew, but they had decided that the elephants were less likely to make a noisy fuss if one of their own kind arrived among them unexpectedly than if two humans did.

It worked. The first elephant in the line snorted violently as Rajah reached out with his trunk and touched it. The others all lifted their heads and, for a dreadful moment Jake was sure they were all going to start trumpeting. Instead they froze and watched with deep interest as he and Dilip unscrewed the bolt holding together the chain around the first elephant's front legs. Lowering the chain gently to the ground so that it made only the softest clank, they moved on to the next animal. While Rajah entwined trunks with it, the boys again crawled between its legs and wrestled with the bolt. As they passed down the line they were aware of the elephants looking at them with rapt interest and it seemed to them that the intelligent creatures knew that they were being freed.

At last they reached the end of the line. None of the elephants had moved as the chain dropped from each leg. Nor had any winced or objected, even though in several cases it must have been very painful for them. There were running sores, some of which stank from infections so that the boys had to hold their breath to stop gagging.

Now it was time to start the stampede. They had decided that, after the warriors had removed as many of the guns as they could without waking the loggers, they would all assemble at the far end of the elephant line. The loggers' camp now lay between the elephants and the forest. The track and the river were behind them and the plan was to scare the loggers into running into the forest and away from the track. Now, according to plan, one of the warriors started to make a strange and very sinister hooting. Quietly at first and then rapidly increasing in volume, it was a horrible, ghostly sound. The elephants began to stir restlessly and figures of men could be seen sitting up around the camp fires and listening.

Then, at a signal, everyone joined in, imitating the hooting or simply shrieking as loudly as they could. This was too much for the elephants who broke away from the line and, their trunks held high in the air, dashed trumpeting towards the camp. Now it was the loggers' turn to start running for the shelter of the trees. Trailing their bedding they floundered barefoot into the undergrowth to escape the stampede, howling with fear. Some paused for a moment to look for their guns only to find that they had vanished.

At the same moment as the elephants started to stampede, and without ceasing to howl and shriek, the warriors all loosed off a volley of stones over the charging animals and into the fleeing men. Now the loggers' howls turned to screams as they heard the stones thud into the ground beside them or hit them on their backs. It was as though there was a sudden massive hailstorm, something mysterious and inexplicable combined with the miraculous escape of the elephants. If any had thought of stopping to halt the charge and try to catch and calm the elephants, the stones changed their minds. Within a few minutes they had all disappeared into the forest and so had the elephants. Shrieks, cries and trumpeting could be heard but the camp was silent.

Now Jake's army moved fast and efficiently, according to plan. A few of the men ran into the camp, gathered up the long chains and dragged them to the river. There they joined the loggers' guns in a deep pool. Even if they were able to catch the elephants, they would now have nothing with which to tether them.

The rest helped to load the saddle bags on Rajah, who had stood quivering with excitement throughout the attack. Jake and Dilip had hung on to an ear each, whispering furiously to him that he must not run off with the others and, reluctantly, he had obeyed them. They made a last check around to make sure nothing had been left behind, and then they were all off down the track, running as fast as they could. It had all gone even better than they could have hoped. As far as they could tell, none of the loggers had seen any of them. All they knew was that there had been a terrible, spooky noise and the elephants had stampeded. Of course they would find some strange little stones all over the place back at the camp when they nerved themselves to return, but this would only add to the mystery. With any luck, the whole incident would have so terrified them and would be built up into such a tall story that it would be a long time before any loggers would dare to return to that forest, whatever the rewards.

The grey mist of dawn was just beginning to rise from the river as they raced along the track together. They kept going until, within a surprisingly short space of time, they saw the outpost at the edge of the reserve. A curl of smoke rose from its chimney, showing that the guard was awake.

'We must say goodbye to them all now,' Jake said to Dilip. One by one the young men came and clasped Jake's hand in both of theirs. They were all laughing and happy, knowing that they had done a good night's work.

'They must get back without being seen,' said Jake and Dilip translated. 'It will be much better if no one ever knows that they were responsible for last night. Also, it will make it easier for them to chase loggers away in the future.'

'They are all asking when they will see you again.'

'Please thank them all for being so brave and for seeing us home safely. Tell them I know we will meet again. Until then, they must look after their forest.'

Suddenly, they were all gone. The boys walked up to the hut and knocked on the door. The guard came out, rubbing the sleep from his eyes. Dilip told him they had been camping happily nearby and thanked him for looking after them so well. At this he looked surprised as he had done nothing, but when Dilip went on to say that he would be asking his father to thank the Chief Ranger for all the help they had received from his guard, he was quite happy to accept that they had been there all the time.

Back at the farm, they handed Rajah back to the old couple, who were very relieved to see them safe and unharmed. With them, too, they covered their tracks by saying they hoped they had received the regular messages sent every day by the guard to say they were all right. Since the couple were not going to land the guard in trouble and the guard had been too lazy to deliver their message to the Chief Ranger, they reckoned no one would ever know what they had been up to. Since they had been up all night, they slept while they waited for Singh to fetch them as planned. Now all they had to do was think of some really good stories to tell Mr and Mrs Barua about their adventures camping in the nature reserve.

Epilogue

Fortunately for Jake and Dilip, the crisis on the tea plantation was still on, even though things were getting better. As a result, Mr and Mrs Barua were not too interested in listening to the stories they told about their time in the reserve. In any case, they had been camping most of the time they had been away so that as long as they kept off the subjects of the village and the loggers they could talk about what had really happened to them.

There was also a message waiting for Jake from his father saying that it was time he went home and so they were all soon talking about his travel plans. Although he liked Dangma and would have enjoyed spending the whole holidays with Dilip, Jake was not unhappy at the prospect of going back to England. He and Dilip would always be friends after what they had been through together and they all agreed that when he was older he would try and come to stay with Jake; but he was beginning to miss his mother, his dog and his home. There was still a lot of the summer holidays left and he wanted to spend them in familiar surroundings.

Granny Maisy was pleased to see him when Jake went and called on her the day after his return. 'I thought you got back last week,' she said, looking confused. 'Didn't you come and see me then?'

Jake guessed that she was remembering seeing him in the dream when she had told him how to find the treasure. 'Don't worry,' he told her. 'I found the treasure in the tree where you hid it. It was quite safe and I did what Grandfather wanted me to do.'

For a moment he thought she was going to cry, like she always had before when her husband was mentioned. But this time she seemed to understand that he was telling her something important. Her eyes cleared and she said, 'Did you really find it? Oh good! I have always felt so guilty that I may not have done what he wanted. Do you promise it's all right now?'

'I promise,' said Jake. 'It's better than all right; it's perfect. And Grandfather would be really pleased.'

'That's wonderful,' replied his granny and a dreamy look began to appear on her face again. 'Wonderful; I'll tell him when I see him. I see him often now, you know . . .' and she closed her eyes and smiled to herself. Jake kissed her and tiptoed out of the room.

❖ Tales of Redwall ❖
BRIAN JACQUES

'Not since Roald Dahl have children filled their shelves so compulsively' *The Times*

An award-winning, best-selling series from master storyteller, Brian Jacques. Discover the epic Tales of Redwall *adventures about Redwall Abbey - and beyond!*

- **Martin the Warrior** 0 09 928171 6
- **Mossflower** 0 09 955400 3
- **Outcast of Redwall** 0 09 960091 9
- **Mariel of Redwall** 0 09 992960 0
- **The Bellmaker** 0 09 943331 1
- **Salamandastron** 0 09 914361 5
- **Redwall** 0 09 951200 9
- **Mattimeo** 0 09 967540 4
- **The Pearls of Lutra** 0 09 963871 1

Tales of Redwall by Brian Jacques
Out now in paperback from Red Fox priced £4.99

ANN COBURN

*B*e warned: where the edges of past and present merge and the borders of time blur... expect the unexpected.

Four very different buddies: Alice, Frankie, David and Michael, have one thing in common - photography. But their passion for cameras is developing into a very dangerous hobby...

1 WORM SONGS   ISBN 0 09 964311 1   £2.99

2 WEB WEAVER   ISBN 0 09 964321 9   £3.50

And coming soon!
3 DARK WATER   ISBN 0 09 964331 6   £3.50

THE BORDERLANDS SEQUENCE by Ann Coburn
Out now in paperback from Red Fox

Book 1
in the
FELIX
TRILOGY

GO SADDLE THE SEA

*A*ction-packed adventure, high-tension
drama and heroic swashbuckling!
*Join dashing hero Felix Brooke as he boldly
embarks upon the journey of a lifetime...
Here's a taster to tempt you!*

'Ye've run yourself into a real nest of adders, here, lad,'
Sammy whispered.

'I know they are smugglers,' I began protesting. 'That
was why the fee was low. But I could take care of my — '

'They are worse than smugglers, lad – they are
Comprachicos,' he breathed into my ear.

'Compra — c-comprachicos?'

At first I thought I could not have heard him aright.
Then I could not believe him. The I *did* believe him –
Sam would not make up such a tale – and, despite myself,
my teeth began to chatter.

THE FELIX TRILOGY by Joan Aiken from Red Fox
Go Saddle the Sea   £3.99   ISBN 0 09 953771 0
Bridle the Wind   £3.99   ISBN 0 09 953781 8
The Teeth of the Gale   £3.99   ISBN 0 09 953791 5